Praise for Mary Roberts Rinehart and
The Man in Lower Ten

"[Rinehart's] literary distinction lies in the combination of love, humor and murder that she wove into her tales. . . She helped the mystery story grow up." *The New York Times*

"Rinehart infuses into her story a lot of humor. Her liveliness of spirit and sprightliness of wit make *The Man in Lower Ten* a distinctive and remarkable work of fiction." *Philadelphia Recorder*

"*The Man in Lower Ten* has a plot that holds the darkest tragedy under a sparkle of romance and comedy… an even more exciting story than *The Circular Staircase*, and the denouement is completely unexpected." *The Argus*

"Rinehart cleverly manages to have the reader know things that the narrator doesn't *and* vice versa." *Edwardian Promenade*

"One of the strangest and most entrancing of latter-day mystery stories… Rinehart's dialogue is crisp and scintillant." *The Sun*

"The rush of incident and the abundance of action, the surprises and the disappointments of the plot lure the reader on and keep the interest at the highest pitch." *The Argus*

The Man in Lower Ten

Mary Roberts Rinehart

Kazabo Publishing

Garamond MT Std 12/16
ISBN: 978-1-948104-26-5
P02

Kazabo Publishing

Kazabo.com

Cover image courtesy of Art-Dreams

Table of Contents

Foreword

Whilom, as olde stories tellen us ther was a duc that highte Theseus.

Language evolves, but great stories are always great stories. Scholars of English literature will recognize the line above as the beginning of the *Canterbury Tales*, some of the best – and funniest – stories ever written in English. But the rest of us will be a lot more comfortable with, *Once, as the old histories tell us, there was a duke named Theseus.*

Great literature should not be limited to scholars. It should always be as fresh, as enjoyable, and as accessible as the day it was written. At Kazabo, we have realized that there is a wealth of older English works, typically written in the late nineteenth and early twentieth centuries, that were hugely successful best sellers in their day but have fallen out of fashion. For the most part this is not because of the plots of these novels, but because the language has become dated and, often, exhausting. Yes, it is still possible to plow through these books if you are dedicated, but it's real work. And these books were meant to be, above all, *fun*.

That's why, at Kazabo Publishing, we are re-issuing some of these works in "modern" English. Unlike other editions of *The Man in Lower Ten*, this version has been completely re-written so that the style is contemporary and easy-to-read while still preserving Mary Robert Rinehart's distinctive tone. If you've ever found a classic mystery to be tough going, our Modern Reader Editions are for you.

The other "problem" with older novels is that they often include obscure references. Of course, back in 1909, these references were not obscure, they were common knowledge. But nowadays, they can really interfere with our enjoyment of these novels and even our understanding of the plot.

We've put the word "problem" in quotes because these references are actually a feature rather than a bug. *The Man in Lower Ten* is a genuine "historical novel" written by the ultimate expert on the era – someone who lived in 1909! There is no better way to step back into that place and time.

We've addressed this by including short paragraphs at the beginning of chapters that briefly explain any references that might be obscure to modern readers. We have found this approach much more satisfying than long introductions full of random facts and much less disruptive to your reading experience than footnotes. So when you see some italicized text at the beginning of a chapter, be sure to read it!

We hope you enjoy reading the Modern Reader Edition of *The Man In Lower Ten* as much as we enjoyed "sprucing it up" for you.

The Kazabo Team

What's a "Lower Ten?"
Sleeping cars: a blast from the past

The Man in Lower Ten was written in 1909, and the heart of the action takes place on a Pullman sleeping car named *Ontario* between Washington D.C. and Pittsburg. Pullman cars provided sleeping accommodations on board overnight trains and were invented by George Pullman who began building and operating them in 1859.

Pullman cars consisted of a series of folding upper berths which could be folded up to the ceiling during the daytime, and "couch seating" that could be converted to a bed at night. The upper berth was less comfortable than the lower berth, and therefore the least expensive accommodation offered in a Pullman sleeping car.

Each Pullman car was staffed by porters – employees of the Pullman company – who turned the train into an efficiently-managed hotel. Porters kept the cars impeccably clean and were responsible for converting the car from its daytime seating arrangement into a sleeping car at night. Porters even shined shoes, pressed suits, sent telegrams, and delivered meals for passengers. Pullman bedding was even removed and cleaned daily.

When Mary Roberts Rinehart wrote *The Man in Lower Ten*, in 1909, Pullman sleeping cars included a variety of different arrangements. These are the ones that are mentioned in the novel.

Upper Berth and Lower Berth – The traditional arrangement of Pullman cars is the open section, where, during the daytime, passengers were accommodated in comfortable sofa seats. At night, some privacy was provided by a curtain that screened a set of upper and lower berths from the aisle, though, as a single traveler, you would often end up with a stranger in the other berth.

Section – If you wanted a bit more privacy, you could hire a "section" which consisted of both an un upper and a lower berth. That gave you the use of both seats as well as extra luggage space and extra pillows and blankets if desired. Since the upper berth would be kept closed, you'd have more headroom as well. N.B. "Section" is also used in a different technical sense that is quite important to the story. But we'll save that for now and introduce it at the beginning of the chapter where it becomes important.

Drawing Room – The ultimate in Pullman luxury, the drawing room provided a spacious living room with a wide sofa, two movable lounge chairs, private toilet, luggage space and a wardrobe for hanging clothes full length. It accommodated three full length beds at night, including an upper berth type bed that dropped down from the ceiling.

Vestibule – An enclosed space between the end doors of adjacent cars, that allowed the doors to be left open and provide for intercommunication between the cars.

About the Author

Mary Roberts Rinehart (1876-1958) was perhaps the most beloved and best-selling American mystery writer in the first half of the twentieth century. Born in Pittsburgh to the owner of a sewing machine factory, she admits in her autobiography, *My Story*, *"There was never any money in those days."* Her father spent most of his spare time working on inventions. He received a patent for a rotary shuttle for sewing machines but many of his other inventions were less successful. Mary had an early aptitude for writing, becoming a published author at 15, but considered it as a hobby rather than as a career.

After attending nursing school, she married Dr. Stanley Marshall Rinehart, with whom she would have three sons. It was not until the family lost $12,000 in the stock market in 1903 that she took up writing seriously in an effort to help pay the bills.

Rinehart had a string of successes, beginning with *The Circular Staircase* in 1906. Her second book, *The Man in Lower Ten* was such a runaway hit that the berth mentioned in the title, lower ten, became unsalable on Pullman cars for quite some time after its publication. By the time she died in 1958 – her last novel, *The Swimming Pool*, was published in 1952 – she had published three dozen novels and numerous other works. Rinehart was often called "the American Agatha Christie" but that hardly seems fair. If anything, Agatha Christie, who began writing 15 years later, was the British Mary Roberts Rinehart.

Chapter One
I GO TO PITTSBURGH

McKnight is gradually taking over the criminal side of the business, which I never liked, especially since the strange case of the man in berth lower ten, which made me uneasy. That incident involved a network of clues pointing to three different people, shattering your faith in circumstantial evidence.

Whenever I see a terrified defendant in court, it reminds me of the horrifying events on the Pullman car Ontario between Washington and Pittsburgh on September ninth, not long ago.

McKnight could tell the story better, although he can't spell three consecutive words correctly. But, while he has imagination and humor, he is lazy.

"It didn't happen to me, anyhow," he protested, when I put it to him. "And nobody cares for second-hand thrills. Besides, you want the unvarnished and ungarnished truth, and I'm no hand for that. I'm a lawyer."

As for me, I'm also a lawyer, unmarried, and just old enough to dance with the younger sisters of my former acquaintances. I prefer the outdoors and horses over romantic pursuits. My housekeeper, an elderly widow, controls my life.

I'm the most prosaic and least adventurous person among my friends, sticking to routines and avoiding deviations from the norm. Yet, by a strange twist of fate, I found myself entangled in a crime and a love affair, leading to a sensational and surprising journey that ended in my firm's private office.

***

It was really McKnight's turn to travel next, but he declined. It was not the first time he had shirked that summer in order to run down to Richmond, and I was surly about it. But this time he had a new excuse, citing his chronic car sickness while crossing the mountains. Despite my plans for a tournament and a yacht cruise, I couldn't argue with his wide-eyed honesty about his condition.

So I eventually gave up on McKnight and went home to pack. Later that evening, he arrived with his car, the Cannonball, to take me to the station, and he brought the forged notes from the Bronson case.

"Guard them with your life," he warned, "they are more precious than honor. Keep them safe, sew them in your chest protector or wherever you keep valuables. I won't be happy until I see Gentleman Andy behind bars."

He made himself comfortable. He sat down on my clean collars, found my cigarettes and struck a match on the mahogany bed post.

"Where's the Pirate?" he asked, referring to my housekeeper, Mrs. Klopton, known for her fierce eyes and buccaneering nose. I closed the door to the hall and replied, "Keep your voice down, Richey. She's looking for the evening paper to check if it's going to rain. My raincoat and umbrella are waiting in the hall."

He left the damaged collars on the bed and went to the window, staring at the neighboring house's wall.

"It's raining now," he said, closing the window and shutters. Something in his voice made me look up, but he was watching me casually, hands in his pockets.

"Who lives next door?" he asked nonchalantly after a pause. I was packing my razor.

"The house is empty," I replied absentmindedly. "If the landlord would fix it up…"

"Did you put those notes in your pocket?" he interrupted.

"Yes," I replied impatiently. "Along with my certificates of registration, baptism, and vaccination. Anyone who wants them will have to steal my coat."

"Well, I'd move them if I were you. Somebody in the next house seemed quite interested in where you put them. Someone right at that window opposite."

I scoffed at the idea but followed his advice, stowing the papers deep in my traveling bag. McKnight looked uneasy. "I have a feeling you're going to have trouble," he said as I locked the bag. "I don't like starting anything important on a Friday."

"You don't like starting anything on any day," I retorted, still upset about missing my Saturday plans. "And if you knew the owner of that house like I do, you'd know he's paying rent for the privilege of peeking through that window."

Mrs. Klopton knocked on the door and spoke discreetly from the hall, "Did Mr. McKnight bring the evening paper?" she inquired.

"Sorry, Mrs. Klopton, I didn't bring the evening paper. The Cubs won, three to nothing," McKnight called out, grinning, as she rustled away in her black silk gown, irritated by the news of the Cubs' win.

With my packing done, collar changed, and the lights off, we cautiously opened the shutters. The window across remained dark and dirty, but Richey's suggestion made me feel like I was being watched.

"We'll have to run for it," I said in a whisper. "She's down there with a package of some sort, sandwiches probably. And she's threatened me with overshoes for a month. Ready now!" We prepared to run past Mrs. Klopton and Euphemia, the housemaid.

"Sorry, no time, be back on Sunday," I quickly informed them as we hurried out the door and into the car.

As we drove away, McKnight focused on the empty house's facade next door. "By George, I'd like to hold a post-mortem on that corpse of a house."

"Probably someone after the brass pipes. The house has been vacant for a year," I dismissed the idea.

McKnight remained sullen, not speaking until we reached the station. With five minutes to spare, we smoked and lounged in the train shed. My mind wandered to a polo pony I couldn't afford but wanted to buy. Then McKnight broke his silence.

"For heaven's sake, don't look so martyr-like," he burst out, "I know you've done all the traveling this summer and you're missing a game tomorrow, but I have to go to Richmond on Sunday… I want to see a girl."

I replied politely, "Don't worry about me; I wouldn't trade places with you. What's her name? North? South?"

"West," he snapped. "Don't try to be funny. And mark my words, Blakeley, if you ever fall in love, I hope you make a complete fool of yourself."

As events unfolded, this statement proved to be oddly prophetic.

***

The trip west was uneventful. I played bridge with some fellow passengers, won three out of four rubbers, and went to bed at one o'clock. It was getting cooler, and the rain had stopped. At one point, I woke up with a start, feeling like someone had been watching me, the same sensation I had experienced earlier in the evening at the window, but I found the bag with the notes by my side, which reassured me, and I went back to sleep.

Later, when I tried to piece together the fragments of that journey, I remembered that my coat, which had been folded and placed beyond my restless tossing, had been rescued in the morning from a heterogeneous jumble of blankets, evening papers and cravat. It occurred to me the necessity of writing a letter of complaint to the Pullman Company about their cramped accommodations. I even formulated some of the letter: "If they are built to scale, why not take a man of ordinary stature as your unit?" I wrote mentally, "I can not fold together like the traveling cup with which I drink your abominable water."

However, after a cup of coffee in Union Station, I felt more cheerful.

As I read the morning papers, I saw they had caught wind of my visit and its purpose. The forged papers in the Bronson case being brought to Pittsburgh were making headlines. Underneath, a telegram from Washington stated that Lawrence Blakeley, of Blakeley and McKnight, had left for Pittsburg the night before, and that, owing to the approaching trial of the Bronson case and the illness of John Gilmore, the Pittsburg millionaire, who was the chief witness for the prosecution, it was supposed that the visit was intimately concerned with the trial. I hoped to avoid reporters, and luckily, none were around as I paid for my breakfast and left the restaurant.

I picked a decent-looking hansom cab at the stand and gave the driver the address of the Gilmore residence in the East end. Just in time, we drove off, leaving a slim young man in a straw hat trying to catch up to us, probably a reporter. I prefer to steer clear of reporters since they can easily trick me into revealing more than I should.

It was about nine o'clock when I left the station. We drove along a boulevard that hugged the side of one of the city's great hills. Far below, to the left, lay the railroad tracks and the towering stacks of the mills, creating with their smoke a haze of grays and blacks, occasionally illuminated by flashes of fire. It was an ugly, tremendous sight. Whistler might have captured its pathos and majesty, but what he would have missed was the essence of its significance: the rattle and roar of iron on iron, the rumble of wheels, the throbbing beat of fire and heat, forging prosperity.

I shared my observations with the grim old millionaire, who bore responsibility for at least part of this industrial landscape. He was propped up in bed at his East end home, listening to the market reports read by a nurse. He smiled slightly at my enthusiasm.

"I can't see much beauty in it myself," he said. "But it's our badge of prosperity. Pittsburg without smoke wouldn't be Pittsburg, any more than New York without prohibition would be New York. Sit down for a few minutes, Mr. Blakeley. Now, Miss Gardner, Westinghouse Electric."

The nurse resumed her reading in a monotonous voice, using initials and abbreviations as they came, without understanding. However, the shrewd old man followed her easily. Once, he corrected her pronunciation, saying, "D-o is ditto, not *do*."

As the nurse continued, I found myself studying a photograph in a silver frame on the bedside table. It was a picture of a girl in white, her hands loosely clasped before her. Against the dark background, her figure stood out as slim and young. Although I generally didn't find photographs of young girls appealing, this one intrigued me. I kept glancing back at it and managed to discern the name written across the corner, "Alison."

Mr. Gilmore observed me under his heavy eyebrows. After the reading was over, and we were alone, he pointed to the picture. "I keep it there to remind myself that I am an old man," he said. "That is my granddaughter, Alison West."

I expressed the customary polite surprise, and he seemed pleased with my response. He told me his age with a chuckle of pride, and our conversation meandered to various topics, including his eating habits and reserve power at the age of sixty-five. Eventually, we circled back to the photograph.

"Father was a rascal," John Gilmore said, picking up the frame. "The happiest day of my life was when I knew he was safely dead in bed and not hanged. If the child had looked like him, I… Well, she doesn't. She's a Gilmore, every inch. Supposed to look like me."

"Very noticeably," I agreed soberly.

By that time, I had produced the notes, and Mr. Gilmore replaced the picture to examine them. He carefully went over each note, scrutinizing them one by one before leaning back and removing his glasses.

"They're not so bad," he said thoughtfully. "Not so bad. But I never saw them before. That's my unofficial signature. I am inclined to think... To think that he has got hold of a letter of mine, probably to Alison. Bronson was a friend of her rapscallion of a father."

I took Mr. Gilmore's statement and kept it along with the forged notes in my traveling bag. When I saw them again, almost three weeks later, they were unrecognizable, reduced to charred paper on a copper ashtray. In the intervening time, more significant events had unfolded, and the Bronson forgery case took a backseat to the greater and more pressing mystery of the man in lower ten. Moreover, Alison West had entered both the story and my life.

Chapter Two
A TORN TELEGRAM

HOT BOX – When an axle bearing overheats on a piece of railway rolling stock, it is called a "hot box." Leaking oil caused the bearings to overheat which could start a fire that might destroy the entire railroad car if not detected early enough.

SECOND SECTION – When a train needed more space for freight or passengers, multiple trains were used on the same route. These trains traveling on the same route were defined as "first section," "second section," "third section," and so on, to differentiate the trains. The "first section" was not always traveling first, but this naming and travel sequence was generally followed by convention.

I lunched alone at the Gilmore house and immediately headed back to the city. The sun had cleared the mists, and a refreshing summer breeze swept away the smoke. The boulevard was bustling with cars heading to the countryside for the Saturday half-holiday, seeking golf, tennis, green fields, and lively company. I couldn't help but think about McKnight visiting the lady with the geographical name in Richmond. It was the first time I connected John Gilmore's granddaughter with McKnight's irritable "West" remark.

I still had my travelling bag with me, a result of McKnight's warning when he saw the empty house. I didn't transfer the notes to my pocket, but even if I had, it wouldn't have changed the situation later.

Only recently, McKnight brought up this very topic. "I warned you," he reminded me. "I told you to be on your guard, as strange things were coming. You should've taken your revolver."

"A revolver would've been useless," I replied. "Whether I stayed awake the whole time or kept my finger on the trigger, the outcome would've been the same. And if you want some excitement, I can guide you to it. It starts with getting the wrong berth on a Pullman car and ends…"

"I know how it ends," he interrupted. "You think the whole thing's not etched into my memory?"

But I digress. That's the trouble with an amateur storyteller; they meander and lose focus. They discard characters when they're done with them and forget important details. And if they add a love affair, they give a sigh of relief when the characters reach the happily-ever-after in the final chapter.

The rest of the afternoon was entirely unsatisfactory. Time dragged on endlessly. I attended a summer vaudeville show and bought some ties at a haberdasher's. I was bored and unprepared, oblivious to what was about to unfold. Unusual occurrences had never been a part of my life; any adventures my friends had were usually tied to women. "Ergo," I always said, "no women!" I repeated this to myself almost savagely that evening when thoughts of John Gilmore's granddaughter crept back into my mind, while I was having a lonely dinner at a downtown restaurant.

"Do you really need more troubles?" I asked myself. "Is your house not in order? Do you want to sell a polo pony just to redecorate the library in mission style or the drawing-room in gold? Do you wish someone to count the empty cigarette boxes lying around every morning?"

Blame it on the long idle afternoon or the new surroundings, but I started to believe that perhaps I did want something more. I felt terribly lonely. For the first time, my steady life seemed uncertain, and the matrimonial seismograph recorded vague but noticeable shifts.

My alligator bag remained locked at my feet. While waiting for my coffee, I leaned back and casually observed the people around me. There were the usual couples engrossed in each other, and my newfound mindset made me view them with understanding.

However, the atmosphere at the next table, where a man and woman dined together, struck me as different. The woman's face captured my attention as she spoke earnestly across the table, her profile facing me. She wore somber clothes and had a striking mass of unusual bronze-colored hair. But it was her expression, filled with hopelessness and almost tragedy, that shocked me. She glanced toward me briefly, then turned back to the man across the table.

Neither of them seemed interested in eating. The man slouched in his chair, chin on his chest, with heavy folds of flesh hanging over his collar. He was probably around fifty, bald, grotesque, and moody, yet not devoid of a sense of power. It was evident that he had been drinking; I noticed him signal a waiter for the wine list raising an unsteady hand.

The young woman leaned closer across the table and spoke quickly, her voice unintentionally rising. Despite her lack of beauty, her earnestness and tension intrigued me. I briefly considered advising the waiter to remove the wine bottle from their table. I wonder what might have happened if I had. What if Harrington had not been intoxicated when he boarded the Pullman car Ontario that night?

It seemed they were about to embark on a journey, and the young woman wanted to go alone. I drank three cups of coffee, which probably contributed to my later restlessness, and shamelessly observed the scene before me. Her protest seemed futile as the man across the table responded with monosyllabic grunts, growing increasingly moody and sullen. During a brief, unexpected lull in the background music, her voice reached me sharply:

"If only I could see him in time!" she said. "It's terrible!"

Although I found the incident intriguing, I would have likely forgotten it right away, discarding it like insignificant clutter in my memory, if I hadn't encountered them again later that evening at Pennsylvania Station. Their situation hadn't visibly changed: the man's determination remained steadfast, but the young woman – his daughter or wife, I wondered – had lowered her veil, leaving me to imagine the profound distress hidden beneath.

While waiting in line with about eight or ten people to buy my berth, a tall woman, whom I hadn't noticed before, spoke to me from my side. She held a ticket and money in her hand.

"Can you please try to get me a lower berth when you purchase yours?" she asked. "I've been in upper berths for three nights."

I agreed to help her and barely paid much attention to her appearance. There was a vague sense of her being tall and dignified, but the crowd behind me was pushing, and someone accidentally stepped on my foot. I obtained two lower berths without difficulty and, with the change and tickets in hand, I offered her a choice.

"Which one would you like? Lower eleven or lower ten?" I inquired.

"It doesn't matter," she replied. "Thank you very much."

Randomly, I handed her lower eleven and called a porter to assist her with her luggage. I followed them leisurely to the train shed, and ten minutes later, we were on our way.

Upon entering my car, I noticed the usual unappealing appearance of sleepers. The berths were already made up, and the aisle was narrow, bordered by dreary curtains that attempted to fend off the breeze. The two seats at each end of the car were cluttered with suitcases and umbrellas. The perspiring porter was doing his best to handle multiple tasks simultaneously.

Nine-fifteen was an unreasonable hour to go to bed, particularly because I rarely sleep or rest on trains. So, I made my way to the smoker car and spent the time until almost eleven with cigarettes and a magazine. The car felt stuffy. Before retiring, I stood in the vestibule for a while. The train had been making frequent stops, and I asked the brakeman what was the trouble. He explained that there was a hot-box on the next car, causing not only our train to run late but also delaying the second section right behind us.

As the night air cooled while we entered the mountains, I began to feel pleasantly drowsy. I bid the brakeman goodnight and returned to my berth. To my surprise, lower ten was already occupied: a suitcase was protruding from beneath the berth, a pair of shoes rested on the floor, and I could hear deep, unmistakable snores coming from behind the curtains. I promptly sought out the porter, and together, we investigated the situation.

"Are you asleep, sir?" the porter asked, leaning over respectfully. Receiving no response, he opened the curtains and looked inside. The intruder was deeply asleep, and the overpowering smell of whisky suggested he would likely remain that way until morning.

I was annoyed; the car was full, and I didn't want to surrender my berth to this drunken intruder and settle for an upper. "You'll have to get out of here," I said, shaking him in frustration. But he only grunted and turned over. As he shifted, I saw his face for the first time: it was the same quarrelsome man from the restaurant.

Now I was more determined than ever to hold onto my spot, but the porter offered a solution to the problem after a discreet investigation. "There's no one in lower nine," he suggested, pulling open the curtains across from us. "He probably belongs in nine, but his condition led to a mistake. You'd better take nine, sir."

I followed his advice and settled into berth number nine, firmly deciding that if the rightful owner appeared later, I'd feign sleep just as soundly as the man opposite me. After putting my shoes out for the porter to polish, and stowing my collar and scarf in the little hammock swung for the purpose, I ensured the forged notes were secure. Then I positioned my pillows for a comfortable view out the window and prepared to gradually drift into sleep.

However, sleep eluded me. The train made frequent and grating stops, presumably due to the hot box issue. While I'm not a nervous person, the thought of the second section trailing closely behind sent a chill down my spine. At one point, as I was dozing, our locomotive sounded a shrill warning: "You keep back where you belong," it screamed in my drowsy ears, and a humbled "All-right-I-will" responded from somewhere behind.

My nerves grew more on edge. At Cresson, I propped myself up on my elbow and gazed at the station lights. Some passengers boarded the train, and I overheard a woman's soft, melodic southern voice. Then all was quiet again. Time passed – perhaps ten minutes, maybe half an hour. Then, without any warning, as the train negotiated a curve, a hefty body was thrown into my berth. It was a startling moment, for despite my attentive ears, I hadn't heard a single step outside. In an instant, the curtain hung still again; my disturber had silently vanished into the darkness. Consumed with restlessness, I sat up, slipped on a pair of slippers, and reached for my bathrobe.

From a berth across, probably lower ten, came that infuriating snore, starting softly like a delicate soprano, descending with each breath, and culminating in an explosive eruption that ripped through the air. My irritation grew, and I sat on the edge of my berth, wishing the snorer would choke. Unfortunately, he seemed to have an unyielding vitality, enduring one bout of snoring after another.

In a desperate attempt to escape the noise, I gathered some cigarettes and a single match, piled my blankets over my bag, and concealed the empty berth by drawing the curtains together. Then I made my way to the vestibule of the train car.

I wasn't exactly dressed for a formal gathering. Why is it that men, constrained to dull attire during the day, prefer to flaunt vibrant colors in their pajamas and dressing gowns? My red and yellow bathrobe, a Christmas gift from Mrs. Klopton, was certainly eye-catching, to say the least.

As I stood there, a feminine figure appeared on the platform. My immediate reaction was to avoid any interaction, but she was quicker than me. She glanced at me with surprise, then swiftly disappeared into the next car, her bronze-colored braids flashing behind her.

With a cigarette in one hand and a match in the other, I leaned against the doorframe and watched her figure disappear. The mountain air flapped my bathrobe around my ankles, the match burned out, but I couldn't take my eyes off her. There was an unmistakable look of horror on her expressive face. I'm no psychologist, but I can sense a woman in trouble, and she was more than troubled; she was in absolute fear.

I hesitated to follow her, fearing my eccentric appearance would only make things worse. A disheveled stranger in a red and yellow bathrobe chasing after her and offering to protect her might not put her completely at ease. *O tempora! O mores!* I recalled a previous incident when I managed to frighten a parlor maid into a week-long seclusion. So, I convinced myself that her distress was either my imagination or my unintentional doing and tried to forget about her. Maybe she was just worried about the unsavory man at the restaurant. I could have easily told her all about him, that he was sleeping soundly in my rightful berth, snoring with an enthusiasm that only the truly intoxicated can muster.

We passed Harrisburg as I stood there. It was a starlit night, and the towering Alleghenies had turned into gentle hills. We passed by several farms, comfortable places that, as McKnight would say, hosted much less comfortable people.

Feeling sleepy and with the image of the woman with bronze hair and fear-struck face fading away, I decided to head back inside. As I turned, a piece of paper fluttered down and landed on my sleeve like a butterfly on a colorful blossom. I picked it up and examined it: it was a torn piece of a telegram. Only fragments of four words were left on the scrap, but they intrigued me. It said, "—ower ten, car seve—."

"Lower ten, car seven," was the berth I had paid for, the one that was taken when I arrived.

Chapter Three
ACROSS THE AISLE

With no solution to that mystery in sight, I returned to my berth. The snorer across seemed to have quieted down, and eventually, I fell asleep, only to be awakened by the morning sunlight on my face.

Still groggy, I reached for my watch, but it wasn't there. Instead, I felt something scratch the back of my hand. Annoyed, I nursed my wound, which was bleeding a little. I checked under the pillow, searching for what I thought might be my scarf pin, but it was gone too. Fully awake now, I reached for my traveling bag, hoping my watch was inside. However, I realized that the bag I held wasn't mine at all. Mine was of alligator hide – I had killed the beast in Florida, after the expenditure of enough money to have bought a house and enough energy to have built one – but this bag was a black sealskin one!

Panicking at the loss of my bag and its important contents, I pressed the bell repeatedly until the porter arrived.

"Did you ring, sir?" he asked, poking his head through the curtains with deference.

"No," I retorted, "the bell rang itself. Why did you switch my bag for this one? Find it immediately, even if you have to wake the entire car. There are crucial papers in that bag!"

From a nearby upper berth, a woman's voice called out impatiently for the porter.

"Let her hang," I said angrily. "Just find my bag."

The porter looked offended and said, "I brought in only your overcoat, sir. You carried your own bag."

He was right! Out of caution, I had refused to give up my alligator bag. It became clear that I had fallen victim to the usual sleeping car theft. By then, I was sweating profusely, and the woman down the car was still complaining. Closer to me, another female voice was giving rapid orders in French, presumably to her maid. The porter was on his knees, searching under the berth.

"It's not there, sir," he said, brushing off his knees. He seemed relieved to be absolved of any responsibility. "I reckon it was taken while you were wandering around the car last night."

"I'll give you fifty dollars if you find it," I offered, "in fact, make it one hundred doll--" I came to an abrupt stop. My eyes were fixed in stupefied amazement on a coat hanging from a hook at the foot of the berth. Then they wandered dazedly to the soft shirt and the collar and cravat in the net hammock across the windows.

"A hundred!" the porter repeated, showing his teeth. I caught him by the arm and pointed at the coat. "What color is that coat?" I asked, unsteady.

"Gray, sir," he replied, gently reproachful.

"And the trousers?"

He held up one creased leg. "Gray, too," he grinned.

"Gray!" I couldn't believe it, even with his confirmation. "But my clothes were blue!"

The porter seemed amused, and he dove under the curtains to retrieve a pair of shoes. "Your shoes, sir," he said with a flourish. "I reckon you must have been dreaming."

Now, you must know that avoiding red neckties and tan shoes is a quirk of mine, call it a bachelor's idiosyncrasy. Yet, there they were — the shoes on the floor were a vibrant yellow, and the scarf in the collar was gaudy red. It took a moment for the reality to sink in. In frustration, I kicked at the offending outfit.

"They're not mine, none of them," I snarled. "They belong to someone else. I'd rather sit here forever than put them on."

The porter admired the clothes, eyeing the red tie with appreciation. "They're nice looking clothes," he remarked. "Not everyone would have left you something."

"Call the conductor," I instructed him shortly. Then a possible explanation struck me. "Oh, porter — what's the number of this berth?"

"Seven, sir. If you can't wear those shoes…"

"Seven!" I almost shouted in relief. "That's it! I'm in the wrong berth. Mine is number nine. But where on earth is the man who should be here?"

"Likely in nine, sir." The porter was enjoying himself. "You and the other gentleman must have gotten mixed up during the night. That's all, sir." He clearly suspected I had been drinking.

Taking a deep breath, I realized that was the explanation. This was number seven's berth – his hat, umbrella, coat, and bag. My anger turned into irritation with myself.

The porter moved on to the next berth, calling out softly, "Time to get up, sir. Are you awake? Time to get up." There was no response from number nine. I suspected he had opened the curtains and looked inside. Then he returned.

"Number nine's empty."

"Empty! You mean my clothes aren't there?" I demanded. "My bag? Why won't you answer?"

"You ain't giving me a chance," he retorted. "There ain't nothin' there. But it looks like someone slept in it."

My brief hope was crushed. Fuming, I dressed in the clothes left for me, including the annoying tan shoes. The porter kept coming back, pretending to be helpful while secretly amused by my distress. When I emerged with the red tie in my hand, he couldn't resist making a sarcastic remark.

"I bet the owner of those clothes looked just as bad as you do in them," he said, wielding the ever-present whisk broom.

"When I find the owner," I replied with determination, "he'll need a burial."

I demanded to see the conductor. He told me that he was on his way, and that there was no bag matching my description on the train. In a hurry, I washed, struggled to fit my neck into a too-small collar, and I hobbled back to the car, for one of the shoes was abominably tight.

Daylight was gradually filling the space, revealing the passengers. Among them was a young woman in blue, with a face I couldn't forget. I had an instant impression that I had met her somewhere, under different circumstances, more cheerful ones, I thought, for the girl's dejection now was evident. Beside her, sitting down, a small dark woman, considerably older, was talking in a rapid undertone. The girl nodded indifferently now and then. I thought, although I was not sure, that my appearance brought a startled look into the young woman's face.

I took a seat, staring ruefully at the other man's shoes. The stage was set. In a moment the curtain was going up on the first act of the play. I felt like the villain in that play, waiting for my lines while the audience hissed.

The porter was trying to wake the occupant of lower ten, but there was no response. He looked at me and winked before pulling back the curtains. Suddenly, his face turned pale, and he muttered in shock. When he stepped back, the interior of lower ten was exposed to the daylight.

The man lying in lower ten was on his back, his face illuminated by the early morning sun. But the light had no effect on him. A small red stain marred the front of his pajamas and trailed across the sheet. His half-open eyes stared blankly at the wood above, unseeing.

I gripped the porter's trembling shoulders and looked down at the lifeless figure. "Good Lord," I exclaimed, "the man has been murdered!"

Chapter Four
NUMBERS SEVEN AND NINE

Afterward, when I tried to recall our discovery of the body in lower ten, my most vivid impression wasn't from the revelation of the opened curtain. It was of a slender girl in a blue gown, seemingly sensing my words rather than just hearing them, with hands tightly clutching the seat beside her. The girl in the aisle stood, leaning toward us, her face showing perplexity and alarm.

The porter nervously attempted to draw the curtains together, but he ended up collapsing on the edge of my berth in shock. I urged him to keep his composure, warning about causing a scene and upsetting the other passengers. Meanwhile, a man nearby, who had been reading yesterday's paper, curiously approached us. He discreetly peeked between the partly open curtains, closed them, and returned to his seat, pretending to be solemn. The atmosphere in the car grew tense; everyone sensed that something was wrong.

After closing the curtains, the porter regained his composure. "It's my last trip in this car," he remarked heavily. "There's something wrong with that berth. Last trip the woman in it took an overdose of some sleeping stuff, and we found her dead! And it isn't more than three months now since there was twins born in that very spot. No, sir, it ain't natural."

At that moment, a thin man with prominent eyes and a gray goatee approached me. He seemed to be a doctor.

"Porter sick?" he inquired, as he noticed the porter's distressed face, my excitement, and the slightly open curtains of lower ten. He checked the porter's pulse with an old-fashioned gold watch.

"Did you have a shock?" he then asked me, to which I replied, "Yes, we both did. If you are a doctor, could you please examine the man in the berth across, lower ten? I fear it may be too late, but I'm not experienced in such matters."

Together, we opened the curtains, and the doctor took a brief but thorough look at the lifeless body and the stains on the sheet. Death was evident in the pallor of the nostrils, the colorless lips, and the absence of the previous night's troubling features. With newfound dignity, the face appeared quite handsome, with abundant gray hair and well-defined features.

The doctor straightened up, facing me. "Dead for a while," he stated, examining the stains professionally. "These are dry and darkened, and rigor mortis is well established. A friend of yours?"

"I don't know him at all," I replied. "Only saw him once before."

"Then you don't know if he was traveling alone?"

"No, he was not... I mean, I don't know anything about him," I corrected myself. It was my first mistake: the doctor looked at me quickly and then returned his attention to the body. Suddenly, I had recalled the woman with bronze hair and a tragic face whom I encountered in the vestibule between the cars in the early morning hours. I had acted impulsively, attempting to protect her as a gentleman would.

The doctor had unfastened the jacket of the striped pajamas, revealing a small punctured wound on the left side.

"It's a precise shot, right through the intercostal space – no time to even grunt."

"Isn't the heart somewhere around there?" I inquired. The medical man turned to me and smirked.

"That's where it belongs, right under that puncture, unless it's gallivanting around a man's throat or his boots."

I gained newfound respect for the doctor, for anyone, indeed, who could crack a joke under such circumstances, or calmly examine the wound and stains. It's strange how healthy people usually hold the medical profession in mild contempt until they fall ill or encounter emergencies like this. Then they meekly turn to those who understand their physical vulnerabilities.

"Is it suicide, doctor?" I asked.

Standing upright, he covered the man's face with the bed-clothing and removed his glasses, wiping them slowly. "No, it's not suicide," he declared firmly. "It's murder."

Of course, I had anticipated that, but hearing the word itself sent a shiver down my spine. I felt a bit dizzy. Curious faces in the car looked our way, and I heard the porter behind me breathing heavily. A stout woman in a negligee walked down the aisle, confronting the porter with irritation. She wore a pink dressing-jacket and held some of her clothing.

"Porter," she began, in the tone of someone who had been inconvenienced, "is there some rule that allows a woman to occupy the dressing-room for an hour, curling her hair, while respectable people have nowhere to even hook their…" Her voice trailed off, and she stared into lower ten. Her once rosy cheeks turned pale, and her jaw dropped. I remember trying to think of something to say but ended up saying nothing at all.

Then, the woman buried her eyes in the nondescript garments hanging from her arm and hurried back the way she came. Gradually, a small group of men gathered around us, mostly silent. The doctor was searching the berth when the conductor pushed his way through, followed by the curious man who had called him. For a while, I lost sight of the woman in blue.

"Did he do it himself?" the conductor asked, taking a businesslike look at the body.

"No, he didn't," the doctor replied. "There's no weapon here, and the window is closed. He couldn't have thrown it out, and he didn't swallow it. What on earth are you looking for, man?"

Someone was on the floor at our feet, face down, peering under the berth. Now he stood up without apologizing, revealing the man who had called the conductor. He looked dusty, alert, and cheerful, and was dragging the dead man's suitcase with him. Seeing it reminded me of my own situation.

"I don't know if there's any connection," I said to the conductor, "but I'm a victim too, to a lesser degree. I've been robbed of everything I had, except a red and yellow bathrobe I happened to be wearing. Whether the thief decline to take that out of delicacy or disgust, I can't say."

A fresh murmur arose in the crowd, and someone nervously laughed. The conductor seemed irritated.

"I can't deal with that now," he snapped. "The railroad company is responsible for transportation, not for clothes, jewelry, and morals. If people want to be stabbed and robbed in the company's cars, it's their problem. Why didn't you sleep in your clothes? I do."

I took an angry step forward, but someone touched my arm, urging me to calm down. I understood the conductor's standpoint, and in a legal sense, I had contributed to my own misfortune.

"I'm not trying to hold you responsible," I said as amiably as possible, "and I believe the clothes the thief left behind are as good as my own, if not better. But my valise contained valuable papers, and it's in your interest as well as mine to find the man who stole it."

"Of course," the conductor said shrewdly. "If you find the man who took this gentleman's clothes, you might also find the murderer."

"I went to bed in lower nine," I continued, my mind still occupied with my lost papers," and I woke up in number seven. I was wandering around in the night as I couldn't sleep, and I must have returned to the wrong berth. Anyway, until the porter woke me up this morning, I had no idea of my mistake. During that time, the thief – or maybe the murderer – must have come back, realized my error, and taken advantage of it to further his escape."

The inquisitive man looked at me with narrowed eyes, like a ferret. "Did anyone on the train suspect you had valuable papers?" he asked, while the crowd listened attentively.

"No one," I replied promptly and confidently. The doctor was examining the belongings of the murdered man. The pockets of his trousers held the usual keys and loose change, while a small pearl-handled revolver, commonly used by women, was found in his hip pocket. A gold watch with a Masonic charm had slipped down between the mattress and the window, and a flashy diamond stud remained fastened in the bosom of his shirt. Overall, the personal items suggested a man of some means but without much refinement. The doctor piled them together.

"Either robbery wasn't the motive," he pondered, "or the thief overlooked these things in his hurry."

The latter seemed more plausible when, after a thorough search, we found no wallet and less than a dollar in small change.

The suitcase yielded no significant clues. It contained an empty leather-covered flask, a pint bottle (also empty), a change of clothing, and some collars marked with the initials S. H. On the leather tag attached to the handle was a card bearing the name Simon Harrington, Pittsburgh. The conductor sat down on my unmade berth, across, writing down the name and address. Then, on an old envelope, he scribbled a few words and handed it to the porter, who disappeared.

"That's all I can do," the conductor sighed. "I've had enough trouble on this trip to last a year. They don't need a conductor on these trains anymore; what they ought to have is a sheriff and a posse."

The porter from the next car came in and whispered to him. The conductor got up unhappily.

"The next car's caught the bug too," he grumbled. "Doctor, there's a woman back there with mumps or bubonic plague or something. Will you go back?"

The unfamiliar porter stepped aside. "A lady about the middle of the car," he said, "wearing black, sir, with peculiar copper-colored hair, I believe, sir."

Chapter Five
THE WOMAN IN THE NEXT CAR

- NOTES –

GODEY'S LADY'S BOOK – Godey's Lady's Book, *also known as* Godey's Magazine and Lady's Book, *was a women's magazine with very wide circulation that was published in Philadelphia from 1830 to 1878. It is mostly known for the hand-colored fashion plate that always appeared at the beginning of each issue.*

ÉMILE GABORIAU – Émile Gaboriau (9 November 1832 – 28 September 1873) was a French writer, pioneer of detective fiction. Gaboriau's novel titled L'Affaire Lerouge *is widely considered as the first detective story in France.*

After the conductor and the doctor left, the group around berth lower ten dispersed, forming smaller clusters throughout the car. The porter remained vigilant and I finally relaxed in my seat, trying to recollect the events of the previous night. However, my inquisitive companion had different plans. Having already taken notes on the deceased person's belongings, name and address, and the crime details, he sat down beside me.

"Now, let's talk about the second victim," he said cheerfully. "What's your name and address, please?"

I eyed him suspiciously. "I've lost everything but my name and address," I replied cautiously. "Why do you need them? For some publication?"

"Oh, no, no! Not for publication," he clarified, surprised by my assumption. "Just for my own understanding. I enjoy gathering such data and drawing my own conclusions. It's quite intriguing. Once or twice I've even helped police investigations for my amusement."

I nodded with tolerance. People have their hobbies, just like a man I once knew who collected old colored prints from Godey's *Lady's Book.*

"I follow the inductive method pioneered by Poe and successfully used by Conan Doyle. Have you ever read *Gaboriau*? Ah, you've missed a treat. But let's get down to business. What's the name of our escaped thief and probable murderer?"

"How on earth would I know?" I replied impatiently. "Did he leave his name written in blood somewhere?"

The little man looked hurt and disappointed. "Are you saying the pockets of those clothes are completely empty?" he asked.

The pockets! In all the excitement, I had completely forgotten about the sealskin bag, which the porter had placed at my feet, and I hadn't examined the pockets at all. With the inquisitive man observing and noting down my findings, I emptied the pockets on the opposite seat.

Upper left waistcoat pocket: two lead pencils and a fountain pen. Lower right waistcoat pocket: a matchbox and a small stamp book. Right coat pocket: new gray suede gloves, size seven and a half. Left coat pocket: a gun-metal cigarette case studded with pearls, half-full of Egyptian cigarettes. Trousers pockets: a gold penknife, some money in bills and change, and a handkerchief with the initial "S" on it.

Further search through the coat uncovered a card-case with cards bearing the name Henry Pinckney Sullivan and a leather flask monogrammed with H.P.S., filled with what appeared to be decent whisky.

"His name is evidently Henry Pinckney Sullivan," the cheerful follower of Poe noted. "But his address is still unknown. He's likely blond. Have you noticed how blond men often favor light gray with a touch of red in their scarf? It's a fact, I assure you. I once kept a record of men's summer attire, and ninety percent followed that pattern. Dark men like you tend to prefer navy blue or brown."

I couldn't help but be amused by the man's shrewd observations. "Yes, the suit he took was dark blue," I confirmed.

He smiled happily and continued, "And you wore black shoes, not tan," glancing at my aggressive yellow shoes.

"Correct," I admitted. "Black low shoes and black embroidered hose. If you keep going, you'll soon have a motive for the crime and the murderer's current hiding place. Come back to the smoker with me, and I'll give you a chance to judge if he knew good whisky from bad."

After putting the items back in the pockets, I got up. "I wonder if there is a dining car," I said. "I need something to eat after all this."

At that moment, the young woman whose face was vaguely familiar approached. As she started to speak, she suddenly drew back and blushed. "Oh, I beg your pardon," she said hurriedly. "I thought you were someone else." She looked at my coat with a puzzled expression, and I felt guilty, as if I had accidentally taken someone else's umbrella. My borrowed collar felt tight around my neck.

"I'm sorry," I stammered, "I'm not."

Later, I learned that she had bright brown hair with a loose wave that fell over her ears and dark blue eyes with black lashes, but that's not what matters. One appreciates a person as a whole, not just the sum of their parts.

She noticed the flask and remembered her errand. "One of the ladies at the end of the car has fainted," she explained. "I thought maybe she could use a stimulant."

I immediately picked up the flask and followed her down the aisle. A few women were attending to the woman who had fainted. They had loosened her collar and removed her hairpins, as if that would help. A stout woman was vigorously rubbing her wrists, perhaps trying to work up her pulse. The unconscious woman was the same one for whom I had secured berth lower eleven at the station.

I poured a little liquor clumsily between her lips as she lay back with closed eyes. She choked, coughed, and began to recover.

"Poor thing," said the stout lady. "As she lies back like that, she reminds me of my mother; she used to faint so often."

"It's enough to make anyone faint," added another woman. "Murder and robbery in one night and on one train car. I'm grateful that I always wear my rings in a bag around my neck, even if they get uncomfortable and keep me awake."

The girl in blue watched us with wide, startled eyes. I noticed her growing paler and saw her exchange a quick, apprehensive glance with her travel companion, the small woman I had observed earlier. There was a brief exchange of glances, and then the small woman frowned. I returned my attention to the patient.

She had regained some strength and requested that the window be opened. The train had stopped once more, and the car felt uncomfortably hot. People checked their watches and grumbled about the delay. The doctor entered, remarking about how busy his day was. The amateur detective and the porter kept an eye on lower ten. Outside, the heat shimmered on the tracks, and the car's wood was hot to the touch. A Camberwell Beauty butterfly flitted through the open door, its wings waving erratically as it navigated down the sunny aisle. All around us, there was the tranquility of harvested fields and the serene calm of the countryside.

Chapter Six
THE GIRL IN BLUE

- NOTES -

DAY COACH – An ordinary passenger-car with normal double seats, as opposed to a sleeping-car, drawing-room car, or dining-car.

I was growing increasingly irritable, and the loss of my notes occupied my mind more than the murder. The forced inactivity became unbearable. As the porter didn't find any bag matching mine on the train, I decided to conduct my own search. I scoured each car, inspecting various types of hand luggage, from luxurious English bags to simple wicker ones in the day coach.

Surprisingly, the girl in blue was also on a similar quest ahead of me. She moved through each car, seemingly focused on a mission. We both reached the end of the train without finding our belongings.

She stepped out to the platform, and I joined her. Somewhere ahead, there was the sound of hammering. The girl remained silent, but her profile looked strained and anxious.

"I—if you have lost anything," I began, "I wish you would let me try to help, even if my own search hasn't been successful."

She barely acknowledged me, which was far from flattering. "I haven't been robbed, if that's what you mean," she responded calmly. "I'm just perplexed. That's all."

There was nothing more to say, so I tipped my hat (the other fellow's hat) and started to return to my car. Several train crew members, including the conductor, were conversing in the shadow. At that moment, the swift clang of a breakfast bell sounded from a nearby farm-house, summoning the workers from barn and pasture. I turned back to the girl.

"We might be stuck here for an hour, and I believe there's no dining car on this train. If I recall my younger days, that bell means ham and eggs, country butter, and coffee. If you're willing to take the chance..." I suggested.

"I'm not hungry," she replied, "but maybe just a cup of coffee. Oh, dear, I believe I *am* hungry," she corrected herself. "Only..." she looked behind her and hesitated.

"Your companion can come with us," I offered, without much enthusiasm. But the young woman shook her head.

"She's not hungry, and she probably wouldn't come anyway," she explained. "Do you think we can make it if we run?"

"I have no idea," I said cheerfully. "Any train would be better than this one if it ends up leaving us behind."

"Yes, any train would be better than this one," she repeated solemnly. I found myself captivated by her ever-changing expressions. We had exchanged just a few words, but I felt like I understood the nuances in her voice – a feat I could never achieve when it came to identifying more superficial details about women.

As we walked back together to where the conductor and the porter from our car were in close conversation, my hand subconsciously reached for my cigarette pocket and came out empty. She noticed the gesture and spoke up, "If you want to smoke, go ahead. My big cousin smokes all the time."

I took out the gun-metal cigarette case and opened it. Strangely, this simple action had an extraordinary effect. The girl beside me stopped in her tracks, fixating on the cigarette case with a fascinated stare.

"Is... Where did you get that?" she asked, her voice catching, her eyes still locked on the cigarette case.

"You haven't heard the rest of the tragedy?" I inquired, offering her the case. "It's awfully bad luck for me, but it makes for a good story. You see..."

Just then, the conductor and porter ended their conversation. The conductor approached me, tugging at his bristling gray mustache, and said, "I'd like to talk to you in the car," casting a curious look at the young lady.

"Can't it wait?" I protested. "We're on our way to get some coffee and bacon..."

"I'm afraid breakfast will have to wait," he replied. "I won't keep you long." There was an air of authority in his voice that I didn't appreciate, but considering the unusual circumstances, I didn't argue.

"We'll have to postpone that cup of coffee for a while," I told the girl. "But don't worry, we'll find breakfast somewhere."

As we entered the car, she stepped aside, but I sensed that she was following us. To my surprise, a group of half a dozen men had gathered around berth number seven, where I had slept. The bed hadn't been made yet.

As we walked down the aisle, I noticed a new expression on the faces of the passengers. The tall woman who had fainted was studying my face with narrowed eyes, while the kind-hearted stout woman avoided my gaze and pretended to look out the window. As we moved through the group, I felt it closing around me menacingly. The conductor said nothing but led me directly to the side of the berth.

"What's going on?" I inquired, puzzled but not alarmed. "Do you have some of my belongings? I'd be grateful even for my shoes; these are awfully tight."

Everyone fell silent, and so did I. My heart pounded in my ears as I noticed a pillow turned over, revealing brownish stains on the white case. It took me a moment to realize that the stains were blood, and the faces around me were now filled with suspicion and distrust.

"That looks like blood," I said, my voice vacant. The conductor's response sounded distant, and my head was spinning.

"It *is* blood," he stated grimly.

Trying to appear nonchalant, I looked around. "Even if it is," I protested, "you surely don't think for a moment that I have anything to do with it!"

The amateur detective barged in, holding a scrap of transparent paper and a pencil. "I'd like permission to trace the stains," he eagerly requested. Then, turning to me, he added, "If you could just prick your finger with a pin, needle, or anything..."

"If you don't back off," the conductor snapped angrily, "I'll do some pricking myself. And as for you, sir…" he turned to me. Although I was completely innocent, I must have appeared guilty. I was drenched in cold sweat, and the pounding in my ears made me feel dizzy. "As for you, sir…"

The determined amateur detective made a swift move at the pillow and pushed back the cover. Before our incredulous eyes he drew out a narrow steel dagger which had been buried to the small cross that served as a head. We all gaped at the sight, and a crowd quickly gathered. So, that was what had scratched my hand! I concealed the wound in my coat pocket.

"Well," I said, attempting to sound composed, "doesn't this prove what I've been telling you? The person who committed the murder must have been in this berth and managed to exchange places somehow after the crime. How do you know they didn't switch the tags to make me come back to this berth?" This was an inspiration, and I was pleased with it. "That's what happened, they changed the tags," I insisted.

The crowd seemed to agree, and the doctor, standing beside me, placed his hand on my arm. "If this gentleman committed the crime – which I doubt – than who is the fellow who got away? And why would he leave?" he questioned.

"We're only taking one person's word for that," the conductor retorted with irritation. "I've traveled in these cars a lot, and no one has ever switched berths with *me*."

Someone on the edge of the group proclaimed that from now on, they would travel during daylight hours. I looked up and met the gaze of the girl in blue.

"They're all insane," she whispered softly, and I heard her clearly. "Don't take them too seriously. Don't bother defending yourself."

"I'm glad you believe I'm innocent," I meekly commented, over the crowd. "Nothing else matters at this point."

The conductor pulled out his notebook again. "Your name, please," he demanded gruffly.

"Lawrence Blakeley, Washington."

"Your occupation?"

"Attorney. A member of the firm of Blakeley and McKnight."

"Mr. Blakeley, you claim that you've occupied the wrong berth and have been robbed. Do you have any knowledge about the man who did it?" the conductor asked.

"Only from what he left behind," I replied. "These clothes…"

"They fit you," he responded with quick suspicion. "Isn't that quite a coincidence? You're a large man."

"Good heavens," I exclaimed, feeling my temper rise, "do I look like someone who would wear this type of necktie? Would any sensible man carry purple and green striped silk handkerchiefs? And why on earth would anyone wear shoes that are a full size too small?"

The conductor seemed hesitant. "You have to understand that I'm in a difficult position," he explained. "I only have your word about the berth exchange, and I'm just doing my duty. Are there any clues in the pockets?"

Once again, I emptied the pockets of their contents, and he noted them down. "Is that all?" he asked. "Was there nothing else?"

"Nothing," I confirmed.

"That's not all, sir," the porter interjected, stepping forward. "There was a small black satchel."

"That's right," I admitted. "I forgot about the bag. I don't even know where it is."

The crowd's suspicion resurfaced. I have become accustomed to reading the faces of a jury, seeing their doubt shift to belief and then back to doubt, so I instinctively watched their expressions. I could tell that my forgetfulness had harmed my case, and suspicion was rising once again.

The bag was eventually found a couple of seats away, under someone's raincoat – another dubious circumstance. Was I hiding it? It was brought to the berth and placed beside the conductor, who opened it immediately.

The bag contained the usual travel necessities – extra clothes, collars, handkerchiefs, a bronze-green scarf, and a safety razor. However, the crowd's attention was fixated on a flat, Russia leather wallet with a thick rubber band around it, bearing in gilt letters the name "Simon Harrington."

Chapter Seven
A FINE GOLD CHAIN

The conductor glared at me, accusingly. "Is this just another coincidence?" he asked. "Did the man who left you his clothes, the silk handkerchief, and the tight shoes also give you the spoils of the murder?"

The onlookers had stepped back, and I realized arguing was pointless. Ever seen a fly getting stuck on fly paper, futilely struggling in despair? Well, that was me. I knew proving my identity wouldn't weigh much against the other incriminating evidence. Imprisonment, trial, and the ensuing notoriety and loss of reputation were inevitable. My mind raced through the possible consequences as I extended my hand to take the pocket-book. Then, I drew my arm back.

"I don't want it," I said. "Check inside. Maybe the other man took the money and left the wallet."

The conductor opened it, and the crowd surged forward curiously. To my dismay, the money was still there – five one-hundred-dollar bills, six twenties, along with some fives and ones, totaling six hundred and fifty dollars.

While the amateur detective recorded the note numbers, I felt indifferent. Small things couldn't irritate me anymore. I pictured myself in the prisoner's box, enduring the nerve-wracking trial for murder – the jury selection, the endless cross-examinations, the alternating hope and fear. Despite usually having nerves of steel, I was now on the verge of hysteria.

Collecting myself, I stood tall, ignoring the doubt and distrust emanating from the crowd. Just then, the amateur detective made a discovery. He had delved back into the seal-skin bag, examining the safety razor and the manufacturer's name on the bronze-green tie. Suddenly, his expression changed, indicating that his theory had been disrupted, and he held up for inspection three inches of fine gold chain from the corner of the bag, one end stained with blood!

The conductor reached out for it, but the little man hesitated to hand it over. He turned to me.

"You claim no watch was left with you? Was there a chain like this?" he inquired.

"No chain at all," I grumbled. "No jewelry whatsoever, except plain gold buttons in the shirt I'm wearing."

"Where are your glasses?" he asked abruptly. Instinctively, I touched my eyes, realizing my glasses had been missing all morning without my noticing. The little man smiled cynically and presented the chain.

"I need you to examine this," he insisted. "Isn't it a part of the fine gold chain you usually wear over your ear?"

I hesitated to touch the stained chain, but with a dozen or so suspicious eyes watching, I reluctantly took it in my fingertips, looking at it helplessly.

"Very fine chains can look alike," I managed to say. "This might be mine, but I don't know how it ended up in that seal-skin bag. I only saw the bag this morning."

"He admits he had the bag," someone murmured behind me. "And how did you guess he wore glasses, anyway?" they asked the amateur sleuth.

The detective cleared his throat. "There were two reasons for suspecting it," he explained. "First, the lines of his face drooping and a pensive eye that hinted at astigmatism. Second, the pronounced line across the bridge of his nose and a mark on his ear from the chain."

After his impressive display of theory and practicality, the detective sat down nearby, still holding the chain, with his eyes closed and lips pursed. Everyone in the car sensed that the mystery was about to be solved. At one point, he leaned forward eagerly and examined the chain on the window-sill with a magnifying glass, only to shake his head in disappointment. The others around him also shook their heads, although they were clueless about what was happening.

My ears started pounding again. The group surrounding me appeared frozen in motion, as if hypnotized. The girl in blue looked at me, and amidst the noise, I thought she said she needed to talk to me about something important. The pounding intensified and turned into a scream. The car jerked and splintered, rising beneath my feet. Then it plunged into darkness.

Chapter Eight
THE SECOND SECTION

Ever been torn from your mundane life, thrown into a whirlwind of events, and landed in a grotesque yet horrifying situation that makes you laugh while groaning, feeling the weight of hopelessness? McKnight calls it hysteria and believes no self-respecting man admits to it.

Also, as McKnight puts it, it's like a tank drama. Just as the revolving saw is about to cut the hero to pieces, the second villain blows up the sawmill. The hero goes flying through the roof and lands next to his beloved, who's innocently making daisy chains.

Nevertheless, when I finally reached the safety of home, with Mrs. Klopton concocting strange pharmacy potions that smelled terrible, I staggered to the door, closed it, and returned to bed, where I howled at the absurdity and madness of it all. Laughing while my soul ached, I knew I had to forget about the girl. The loyalty that binds men's honor demanded it.

Yet, throughout that painful night filled with demons of agony, I kept seeing her as she had been last, wearing the peculiar hat with green ribbons. I cautiously mentioned this to the doctor the next morning, and he attributed it to the morphine, saying I was lucky not to have seen green-tailed devils.

As for the wreck on September ninth, I'm clueless. You, who devoured the details with your morning coffee and digested the horrors with your meal, probably know much more than I do. I do recall, however, that my consciousness returned slowly. I thought I was surrounded by clouds, like meringue on a blue charlotte russe. I heard a woman nearby sobbing over losing her hat pin and struggling to keep her hat on.

In and out of consciousness, I witnessed my patch of blue sky turn hazy with smoke, heard strange roars and crackles, and felt fiery sparks rain down on my face. Someone was weakly beating at me. I opened and closed my eyes, and there she was – the girl in blue – bending over me. Despite the chaos, she urgently tried to rouse me, telling me I had caught fire twice already. A piece of striped ticking drifted by, catching fire as the wind whisked it away.

"It looks like a kite, doesn't it?" I said cheerfully. Then, as my arm throbbed excruciatingly, I winced, "Wow, my arm hurts!"

The girl leaned over and spoke slowly, as if addressing a deaf person or a child, "Listen, Mr. Blakeley, you *must* rouse yourself! There's been a terrible accident. The second section crashed into us. The wreck is on fire, and if we don't move, we'll catch fire too. Understand?"

Her voice and the pain in my arm were bringing me back to my senses. "I hear you," I replied. "I'll try to sit up. Are you hurt?"

"No, just bruised. Can you walk?"

I cautiously tested my feet. "They seem okay," I said doubtfully. "By the way, could you tell me where the back of my head has gone? It feels like it's missing."

She checked my head. "It's pretty badly bumped," she said. "You must have fallen on it."

I managed to prop myself up on my uninjured elbow, but the pain forced me back down. "Please, don't look at the wreck," I pleaded with her. "It's horrible. If there's any way to bandage my arm, I might be able to help, there could be people trapped under those cars!"

"It's too late to help now," she replied solemnly. Feathers floated over us from a burning pillow, and part of the wreck collapsed with a crash. Trying to play my part amidst the tragedy, I got to my knees. Then I noticed that the hand and wrist of my broken left arm were stuck through the handle of the sealskin bag. I gasped and sat back down.

"You must not do that," the girl insisted. She kept her back turned to the wreck, averting her eyes. "The weight of the bag must be agony. Let me support it until we move away, and then you must lie down until we can cut it off."

"Will it need to be cut off?" I asked calmly. Despite the red-hot stabs of pain, we were gradually moving away from the tracks.

"Yes," she replied with surprising composure. "If I had a knife, I could do it myself. You should sit here and lean against this fence."

As my senses returned, I realized she was talking about cutting off the bag, not my arm. The dizziness subsided, and I started to regain control.

"If you pull, it might come loose," I suggested. "And without that weight, I might stop feeling like a helpless baby."

She gently tried to loosen the handle, but it wouldn't budge. Finally, with cold sweat dripping, I had to give up. "I don't think I can endure this," I said. "But there's a knife somewhere among these clothes. If I can find it, maybe you can cut the leather."

I gave her the knife, and she examined it with a bewildered expression, more of confusion than surprise. Without saying a word, she skillfully worked on cutting the bag, and in a few minutes, it fell free.

"That's better," I said, sitting up. "Now, if you can pin my sleeve to my coat, it will support the arm, and we can move away from here."

"The pin might not hold, and the sudden jerk would be terrible," she objected. She looked around and then returned with a partially scorched sheet. After tearing it into a large square and folding it, she slipped it under my broken arm and securely tied it at the back of my neck. The relief was immediate, and I picked up the bag, walking slowly beside her, away from the tracks.

The first act was over, the curtain had fallen, and the scene was "struck."

Chapter Nine
THE HALCYON BREAKFAST

Still dazed, we wandered like troubled children, our main goal being to distance ourselves from the horror we left behind. Grimy and pallid, we encountered curious country folks on the way to the track. Some of them wished to ask us questions, but we hurried past them, not wanting to dwell on the wreckage.

At one point, the girl looked back, and I suddenly remembered that she hadn't been alone on the train. Feeling guilty for not considering her traveling companion earlier, I offered to go back and inquire about her. However, she stopped me, suddenly loosing her composure. "Please don't go back," she said. "I am afraid it would be of no use. And I don't want to be left alone."

"Then I won't leave you," I said manfully, and we stumbled on together.

I was more than content to walk along beside her aimlessly, yet, I couldn't ignore my unkempt appearance and the discomfort of my shoes. In contrast, despite her disheveled appearance, the crumpled dress, her missing hat and the small gold bag that hung forlornly from a broken chain, the girl looked lovely.

So far we had seen nobody from the wreck, but as we walked further, we encountered the woman from berth lower eleven, her black hair about her shoulders, disoriented and bruised. She didn't recognize us and refused our company, muttering incoherently, rolling in her hands a dozen pebbles she had gathered in the road.

The girl worried about my bandaged injury. "Does it hurt very much?" she asked. I assured her it was bearable, though it was far worse than I admitted. If anything in this world could be worse, I had never experienced it.

Trudging bareheaded under the scorching sun, we left the smoke pillar behind, growing parched and weary. I thought of the possibility of a trolley line or of finding a horse and trap to reach Baltimore. However, the girl smiled at the suggestion.

"We'll certainly cause a sensation, won't we?" she asked, half-jokingly. "Isn't it strange? I keep wishing for gloves, when I don't even have a hat!"

When we reached the main road, we sat down for a moment. Her hair fell in lovely waves over her shoulders and when she tried to tie it up again I suggested she'd leave it as it was. But she explained that it was bothersome and got in her eyes when left loose. So, I held a row of little shell combs and pins for her to gather it up, and it looked stunning when done. Funny how men only realize they have hair when they start losing it, while it's different for women.

She seemed to grasp the unconventional situation as she finished arranging her hair. "I haven't even told you my name," she said abruptly. "I forgot that you know nothing about me. I'm Alison West, and I'm from Richmond."

So that was it! She was the girl in the photograph on John Gilmore's bedside table, the girl McKnight was expecting to meet in Richmond the next day. She was on her way back to meet him! What did it matter, though? We were thrown together by chance. Soon, we would be back in civilization, and she'd probably remember me as a scruffy guy with a red cravat and tan shoes, wearing a soiled sheet as a makeshift bandage. I took a deep breath.

"Just a twinge," I replied when she looked up quickly. "Thank you for letting me know, Miss West. I've heard wonderful things about you for the past three months."

"From Richey McKnight?" she seemed genuinely curious.

"Yes, from Richey McKnight," I confirmed. No wonder McKnight was in love with her. I kicked at the dust absentmindedly.

"I was visiting near Cresson, in the mountains," Miss West continued. "The person you mentioned, Mrs. Curtis, was my hostess. We were on our way to Washington together." Her words were measured, as if she wanted to share the minimum of details. The perplexing expression of trouble returned to her face.

"You were heading home, I presume? Richey spoke about seeing you," I stumbled, feeling the need to say something.

She looked straight into my eyes. "No," she replied calmly. "I didn't plan to go home. Well, it doesn't matter… I'm going home now."

Suddenly, a woman in a calico dress, accompanied by two identical children, rushed down the road. She quickly assessed the situation and offered her hospitality.

"You poor things," she said sympathetically. "Take the first road to the left over there, and turn in at the second pigsty. You'll find breakfast on the table and a coffee-pot on the stove. Plenty of soap and water, too. Don't worry; there's no one there to see you."

We gratefully accepted the invitation, and she hurried off toward the excitement and the railroad. I carefully helped Miss West to her feet.

"To the second pigsty on the left, where breakfast awaits!" I exclaimed. "Onward to the pigsty!"

The rest of the walk was mostly quiet. I was pushing my endurance to the limit, as with each step, the broken ends of my bone grated together. Thankfully, we found the farm-house without trouble, though I wondered if I could make it to the door at the end of the old stone walk between hedges.

"The Lord be praised," I mustered, trying to sound lively. "Behold the coffee-pot!" Then, I put down the bag and collapsed on the porch floor. When I regained consciousness, I felt something warm trickling down my neck, and a despairing voice was saying, "Oh, I can't seem to pour it into your mouth. Please open your eyes."

"But I don't want it in my eyes," I replied dreamily. "I'm not sure what happened. Maybe it was the shoes; the left one is a red-hot torture." By then, I was sitting up and looking into her face.

I had never fainted before, nor since, but I would gladly do it a dozen times a day to experience again the blissful touch of her soft fingers on my face and the hot ecstasy of coffee spilled down my neck by those very fingers. There was a thrill in every word she spoke that morning.

Before long my loyalty to McKnight would step between me and the girl he loved: life would develop new complexities. In those early hours after the wreck, despite the pain, there was nothing of the suspicion or distrust that would come later. Stripped of our external trappings, we were like primitive beings, man and woman together: our world for that moment was the deserted farm-house, the slope of wheat-field leading to the road, the woodland lot, the pasture.

We had breakfast together at the modest table. Our initial cheerfulness, born out of sheer reaction, became more genuine as we enjoyed thick slices of bread from the granny oven at the back of the house. The hot beverage we drank resembled coffee but had a unique taste unlike anything I had ever experienced. Cream from stone jars and a basket of great yellow-brown eggs were delightful additions.

Like two children roused from a bad dream, we chatted over our meal, sought common acquaintances, and shared laughter over my feeble attempts at humor. We made a conscious effort to put the horror behind us, but the strangeness of the situation lingered, especially when she mentioned her hat with the green ribbons.

Throughout the morning, I noticed Alison West trying to suppress some troubling thoughts that occasionally surfaced. It brought back the puzzled expression I had observed earlier, before the accident. I caught it once, when she was adjusting the sling for my broken arm after breakfast. I had purposely prolonged the meal, but when the clock struck half-past ten, and the woman with the identical children hadn't returned, Miss West reluctantly made the move I had been dreading.

"We should start if we want to get to Baltimore," she said, getting up. "You should see a doctor as soon as possible."

"Hush," I cautioned. "Please don't mention the arm; it's asleep right now. You might wake it up."

"If only I had a hat," she pondered. "It wouldn't need to be fancy, but..." Suddenly, she exclaimed and rushed to a corner of the room. "Look," she declared triumphantly, "here's just the thing. With the green streamers fashioned into a bow, like this... Do you think the child would mind? I can leave about five dollars here; that should buy a dozen of these hats."

The hat was an odd straw creation, with a round crown and a floppy rim. However, as soon as she put it on, it transformed from grotesque to a delightful sight. Clearly, the lack of head covering had been bothering her, so she was thrilled with her discovery. She left me, wrote a note of thanks that she pinned along with some money to the tablecloth, and hurried upstairs to use the mirror and the soap and water we had been promised earlier.

I didn't see her when she returned downstairs. I had found a bench with a tin basin outside the kitchen door and was attempting to wash with only one functional hand. I felt rather than saw her, standing in the doorway, and I joked, "How can a man with only a right hand wash his left ear? There's so much soap on me that I'll blow bubbles if I laugh."

After finishing my improvised cleaning session, I looked at the girl and noticed something was off. She stood against the door frame, her face pale, and she struggled to breathe. The quirky hat was still on, albeit slightly askew. When I realized she wasn't looking at me but past me, to the road along which we had come, I turned to follow her gaze. There was no one in sight on the sunlit, dust-covered lane, no moving figures, no signs of life.

Chapter Ten
MISS WEST'S REQUEST

Her sudden transformation left me speechless. The lively atmosphere at the breakfast table was gone, and she didn't react to my playful banter as she used to. Standing there, her face pale and serious, she stared at the dusty road, clutching something in her hand. She glanced at the object and then to the distant road with a quick breath. Slowly she regained her color. Whatever had caused the change, she said nothing, eager to leave and impatient with my slow packing.

Later, I realized that I wanted to check the barn for a horse or a vehicle to take us to the trolley, but she wouldn't let me. There are many other things that I recalled later and might have helped me understand, but at the time, I was utterly bewildered. Except for the train wreck, the responsibility for which lay between Providence and the engineer of the second section, everything that happened that morning seemed logically connected. Everything came from one cause, and lead to one end. But the cause was buried, the end not yet in view.

Only when we had put some distance between us and the house did the tension ease from the girl's face. Aware of how intently I had been observing her, she turned to me somewhat irritably.

"Please stop staring," she said, catching me off guard. "I know this hat looks awful. Green always makes me look terrible."

"Maybe it was the green," I said, feeling unexpectedly relieved. "A moment ago, you seemed quite pale to me."

She glanced at me briefly, but I kept my gaze forward. Whatever she held in her hand, she never looked at it, but its presence weighed on her every second. While still in sight of the gate, she made a quick decision, murmured something, and turned back alone, moving swiftly. She fastened something to the gate-post with nervous haste. When she joined me again, she didn't explain, but her clenched fingers were now free, and while she looked tired and worn, her tension seemed to relax.

We walked slowly towards the suburban trolley line. A man offered us a lift on a wagon, but seeing as it was springless, I declined, thinking of my broken bones. My companion declined as well, and we continued together. Once, when we could see the trolley line in the distance, she got a pebble in her shoe, and we sat under a tree while she removed it.

"I must say, I'm grateful for your company," I stumbled over my words. "Your moral support and all that. Do you know, after the train wreck, my first thought was relief that you weren't hurt."

Sitting beside me, shaded by a large chestnut tree, I noticed a look of misery on her face, which I certainly hadn't intended to evoke.

"And my first thought," she spoke slowly, "was regret that I hadn't been obliterated, blown out like a candle. Please don't look like that! I'm just talking."

But her lips trembled, and in the midst of her emotional turmoil, I put social formalities aside and gently patted her hand on the grass.

"You mustn't say such things," I protested. "Perhaps, your friends…"

"I had no friends on the train," she interjected, her voice firm and final. She withdrew her hand from mine with determination as a car approached. We were returning to civilization, to propriety, visiting cards and formal introductions. Miss West put her shoe back on.

We remained mostly silent during the ride in the car. Other passengers openly stared at us, discussing the dreadful wreck and its horrors, but the girl seemed oblivious. At one point, she turned to me with the usual grace that was one of her charms.

"I don't want my mother or Richey to know I was in the accident," she confided. "Can you please not tell Richey about having met me?"

Naturally, I promised to keep her secret. As we approached Baltimore, she asked to examine the gun-metal cigarette case and remained silent, holding it, while I recounted the events of the early morning on the Ontario.

"So you see," I concluded, "this bag, and everything I have on, belongs to a fellow named Sullivan. He probably left the train before the wreck, perhaps just after the murder."

"So you believe this Sullivan committed the crime?" she asked, her eyes fixed on the cigarette case.

"Seems likely," I replied. "A man doesn't leave a train in the middle of the night wearing someone else's clothes unless he's trying to escape something. Besides the dagger, there were the blood stains you saw.

And I even have the murdered man's wallet in this bag at my feet. Doesn't that look suspicious?"

A faint smile appeared on her lips, and I blushed slightly. "Well, that is, if you want to believe I'm innocent," I added.

Just then, her small gold purse's chain gave way, but she didn't notice. I picked the purse up and put it in my pocket for safekeeping, promptly forgetting about it. Later, I wished I had left it on the floor of that little suburban car. Even now, when I see a similar trinket, I shudder involuntarily at the memory of the girl's puzzled eyes under her floppy hat and the haunting suspicion of the sleepless nights that followed.

At that moment, my priority was to prevent my companion from dwelling on the wreck, so I tried to be intentionally light-hearted.

"Do you realize it's Sunday?" she suddenly asked, "and we look a complete mess!"

"Never mind that," I replied. "On Sundays, Baltimore falls into three categories: those who rise up to go to church, those who rise up and read newspapers, and those who don't rise up. The first group is somewhere between the creed and the sermon, and we need not worry about the others."

"You treat me like a child," she said, sounding a bit irritated. "Don't force cheerfulness. It's almost in bad taste."

After that, I deflated like a pricked balloon, and the rest of the ride passed in silence. When she mentioned she would go to her friends in the city, I was taken aback, as it meant an earlier separation than I had anticipated. But my arm was starting to hurt again, and when I put her in a cab, the pain made me forget about her gold purse.

She leaned forward and extended her hand. "I may not get another chance to thank you," she said, "I can't express how grateful I am." I mumbled something about the gratitude being mine. Due to the pain, I saw two cabs and two girls with outstretched hands.

"Remember," they both said, "you've never met me, Mr. Blakeley. And if you hear anything unpleasant about me, I hope you'll think the best of me. Will you?"

The two girls merged into one, with little flashes of light around them. "I'm afraid I'll think too highly for my own good," I said, feeling a bit unsteady. The cab drove away.

Chapter Eleven
THE NAME WAS SULLIVAN

- NOTES -
SCIENCE AND HEALTH: SCIENCE AND HEALTH WITH KEY TO THE SCRIPTURES – *First published in 1875 and written by Mary Baker Eddy, is one of the central texts of the Christian Science religion.*

Back in Baltimore, my arm was temporarily taken care of, and I caught the next train home. I was in bad shape when I arrived, almost stumbling into the arms of a shocked Mrs. Klopton. In no time, I was in bed, with her piling on blankets and using hot-water bottles without much protection, causing blisters in odd places. An hour later, Dr. Williams administered chloroform and set my broken bone.

I drifted off to sleep, waking in the dim evening light, realizing I was back home without the papers that could convict Andy Bronson and still facing a murder charge. On top of that, I couldn't shake the enigma of the girl my best friend was in love with.

"I'm terrible at solving mysteries," I sighed aloud. Mrs. Klopton came over and placed a cold cloth on my forehead.

"Euphemia," she called to someone outside the door, "call the doctor and inform him that he's still rambling, but now it's about mysteries instead of green ribbons."

"There's nothing wrong with me, Mrs. Klopton," I protested weakly. "I was just thinking aloud. Blast this cloth, it's dripping all over me!" I flung it away, and it landed with a wet thud on the floor.

"Talking aloud means you're delirious," Mrs. Klopton stated calmly. "A fresh cloth, Euphemia."

This time, she firmly held it in place, and I was too weak to resist. I feebly complained that I was drowning, which she attributed to my mental state, and then I drifted off into a damp sleep.

It was probably midnight when I woke again, dreaming of the train wreck. Feeling the stability of my bed and seeing Mrs. Klopton sitting fully dressed by the night light, reading *Science and Health*, was immensely reassuring.

"Does that book say anything about opening windows on a hot night?" I asked when I got my bearings.

She immediately put the book down and came over to me. Mrs. Klopton is only ever chastened when reading *Science and Health*.

"I don't like opening the shutters, Mr. Lawrence," she explained. "Not since the night you left."

When pressed for more information, she refused to elaborate. "The doctor said you shouldn't be excited," she insisted. "Here's your beef broth."

"Not a drop till you spill the beans," I asserted. "You know there's nothing wrong with me. This arm is just a figment of my imagination." I cautiously sat up. "Now, open that window, will you?"

Mrs. Klopton finally relented. "There are weird happenings in the house next door," she revealed. "If you have the beef broth, Mr. Lawrence, I'll spill the beans, as you say."

The strange happenings, however, turned out to be somewhat underwhelming. It appeared that, after I left on Friday night, a light was spotted flickering sporadically through the vacant neighboring house. Euphemia was the first to see it and alerted Mrs. Klopton. They both anxiously observed it until it vanished on the lower floor.

"You should've been a ghost story writer," I teased while adjusting my pillows.

"The light was indeed flickering," she reiterated. "And what's more, it came back!"

"Oh, come now, Mrs. Klopton," I objected, "ghosts are like lightning; they never strike twice in the same night. That is only worth half a cup of beef broth."

"You may ask Euphemia," she retorted with dignity. "Not more than an hour after, there was a light there again. We saw it through the chinks of the shutters. Only—*this time it began at the lower floor and climbed up!*"

"You oughtn't to tell ghost stories at night," came McKnight's voice from the doorway. "Really, Mrs. Klopton, I'm amazed at you. You old duffer! I've got you to thank for the worst day of my life."

Mrs. Klopton gulped. Then, realizing that the "old duffer" was meant for me, she took her empty cup and went out muttering.

"The Pirate is crazy about me, isn't she?" McKnight quipped as the door closed. Then he turned around and extended his hand. "By Jove," he exclaimed, "I've been making all sorts of efforts to get in touch with you all day. Left lilies on your doorbell, wore black gloves, did everything. If you had even a hint of common sense, you would've called me."

"I never even considered it." Remorse filled me. "Honestly, Rich, all I wanted was to escape from that place. If you had seen what I saw…"

McKnight interrupted me. "Seen it! You crazy person, I've been searching for you all day in the ruins! I've endured horrors during lunch and dinner. I need something strong, Lollie."

He had found the key to the liquor cabinet in my shoe bag and was mixing himself what he called a "Bernard Shaw" – brandy and soda as the base, with a splash of everything else available to give it a kick. As I could now see him clearly, he looked tired and dirty. I dreaded giving him the news he was eagerly waiting for, but there was no point in prolonging it. I took the plunge and got it over with.

"The notes are gone, Rich," I whispered, trying to keep my voice steady.

His expression betrayed disappointment against his will. "I sort of expected it," he sighed. "But Mrs. Klopton mentioned over the phone that you brought home a bag, so I had a glimmer of hope. Well, we can't complain. You're here… injured, but here." He raised his glass. "Here's to better days, old man!"

"If you pass me that black bottle and a teaspoon, I'll drink that in arnica, or whatever the stuff is. Rich, the notes were gone even *before* the accident!"

He turned and looked at me, holding the bottle in his hand. "Lost, strayed, or stolen?" he asked with forced lightness.

"Stolen, though I believe the theft was secondary to something else."

Mrs. Klopton entered the room at that moment, carrying a glass of egg nog. She glanced at the clock and, without addressing anyone directly, hinted that it was bedtime for respectable people. McKnight, always quick with a comeback, spoke to me in a stage whisper. "Is she talking again? Or still?" he inquired, just before the door closed. After a brief moment of hesitation with the doorknob, Mrs. Klopton decided to leave us be.

"Now, spill it," McKnight said, taking a seat beside the bed. "Not about the accident – I know all I need to know about that. Tell me about the theft. I bet you it was a woman."

I had managed to get out of bed painfully and was pouring the egg nog into the sink. I paused, holding the glass in the air. "A woman?" I echoed, surprised. "What makes you think that?"

"You don't understand the basics of a good detective story," he scoffed. "Of course, it was the woman from the empty house next door. You mentioned the brass pipes, remember? Well, onwards with the investigation; let the fun begin."

So I recounted the story, having done it so many times that day that it became almost automatic. I spoke about the girl with the bronze hair and my suspicions, but intentionally omitted mentioning Alison West. McKnight listened without interruption and let out a deep breath when I finished.

"Well," he said, "that's quite a mess, isn't it? If you can prove your innocence and gentle nature, they can't hold you for the murder. But the missing notes – that's a different story. They aren't burned, at least. Your man wasn't on the train, so he wasn't in the wreck. If he didn't know what he was stealing, as you suspect, he probably reads the newspapers, and by now, he's probably aware of what he's got. He'll likely try to sell them to Bronson."

"Or to us," I interjected.

We remained silent for a few minutes. McKnight smoked a cigarette and gazed at a picture of Candida above the mantel. Candida was the finest pony in seven states.

"I didn't go to Richmond," he finally remarked. His words mirrored my own thoughts so closely that I was taken aback. "Miss West hasn't returned from Seal Harbor yet."

As I didn't respond, he sank back into contemplative silence. Mrs. Klopton entered just as the clock struck one, and made preparations for the night, arranging a gaudy, comfortable blanket into an armchair in the dressing-room, with a smaller, stiff-backed chair for her feet. She was quite fashionably dressed in a dressing-gown that seemed to be a fusion of all the ones she had given me over the past Christmases. She had a purple veil covering her head, concealing who knows what imperfection. She checked the empty egg nog glass, asked what the evening paper had said about the weather, and then noisily settled in the dressing-room, making it clear that she intended to sit up all night.

We fell into silence again as McKnight traced a rough sketch of the berths on the white tablecloth, trying to decipher it slowly.

"You believe he switched the tags on berths seven and nine, so you climbed into the wrong one, thinking it was nine, right?" McKnight asked.

"Probably, yes," I replied.

"Then, in the early morning, while everyone was asleep, your theory is that he switched the tags again and left the train."

"I can't think of any other explanation," I responded wearily.

"What a game of bridge that guy would play! It's like finessing an eight-spot and winning. They wouldn't have doubted your story had the tags been reversed in the morning. He really put you in a tight spot. No jury in the country would ignore the bloodstains, the dagger, and the dead man's wallet found in your possession."

"So, you think Sullivan did it?" I asked.

"Absolutely," said McKnight confidently. "Unless you did it in your sleep. Look at the bloodstains on his pillow and the dagger stuck in it. And didn't he have Harrington's wallet?"

"But why did he leave without the money?" I pressed. "And where does the girl with the bronze hair fit in?"

"Beats me," McKnight replied flippantly. "Probably a figment of your imagination."

"Then there's the torn piece of telegram. It mentioned 'lower ten, car seven.' It's very likely she had it. That telegram was about me, Richey."

"I'm getting a headache," he said, extinguishing his cigarette on the sole of his shoe. "All I know for sure right now is that if there hadn't been a train wreck, you'd be sitting in a small jail cell by now, and feeling miserable about it."

"But listen to this," I argued as he picked up his hat, "this Sullivan guy is on the run, and he's more likely to reach out to Bronson than to us. We could request a continuance in the case, get Bronson released on bail, and set a watch on him."

"Not my watch," McKnight protested. "It's a family heirloom."

"You better head home," I said firmly. "Go home and get some sleep. You're tired. If you think it'll help, you can dream about Sullivan's red necktie."

Mrs. Klopton's drowsy voice came from the next room, punctuated by a yawn. "Oh, I forgot to tell you," she called, with her typical nighttime lisp, "someone called around noon, Mr. Lawrence. It was a long-distance call, and he said he'd call again. The name was..." she yawned, "Sullivan."

Chapter Twelve
THE GOLD PURSE

- NOTES -

SEIDLITZ POWDER – Seidlitz powders were a common heartburn remedy. They consisted of two paper envelopes, one blue, one white, that had to be mixed together in water. When they were, they became a bubbly, effervescent drink.

"I AM SADDEST WHEN I SING!" – A popular nineteenth-century ballad about absent friends written by Thomas Haynes Bayly (1797–1839). He was an English poet, songwriter, dramatist and writer.

"ANOTHER LITTLE DRINK" – A dance hall song from the late nineteenth century. Written by Nate D. Ayers, the song was extremely popular and supremely silly, as you can tell from the first stanza and the refrain:

Oh, there was a little hen and she had a wooden leg
The best little hen that ever laid an egg
And she laid more eggs than any hen on the farm
And another little drink wouldn't do us any harm

Another little drink, another little drink
Another little drink wouldn't do us any harm
Another little drink, another little drink
Another little drink wouldn't do us any harm

I always made fun of those cases of instant attraction, where two people are brought together like the components of a seidlitz powder, creating a bubbling and transient ecstasy. But there can be occasions where the connection between two individuals with shared mindset and interests is so powerful, that the bond between them grows stronger even between their first and next meeting. This is especially true for those with temperament, the modern equivalent of imagination. It is an intriguing question whether lovers begin to fall in love when they are together or when they are apart.

Not that I entertained such thoughts at the time. I refused to admit my foolishness, even to myself. However, during the restless hours of the first night after the accident, when my back ached from lying on it and any other position was torture, my mind kept going back to Alison West. I dozed off, dreaming of touching her fingers again to comfort her, and woke up realizing I had inadvertently patted a teaspoonful of medicine out of the hand of an indignant Mrs. Klopton. What was it McKnight had said about me making an ass of myself?

That brought my thoughts back to Richey, and I think I groaned. The bond between two men who have gone through college together, quarreled and reconciled, discussed politics and debated beliefs for years is inexplicable to others. Nevertheless, I groaned. If it had been anyone other than Rich!

However, there were certain things that belonged to me, and I was determined to keep them: the delightful breakfast, the peculiar hat, the pebble in her shoe, the gold purse with the broken chain… the purse! It was still in my pocket at that moment.

I got up painfully and found my coat. Yes, there it was, the purse with a hint of wealth inside. I returned to bed, feeling somewhat dizzy from the effort and the touch of the trinket, which had recently belonged to her. I held it up, admiring it. If I followed the doctor's orders, I should be out in a day or so. Then, I could return it to her. I really should do that; it was valuable, and I wouldn't trust it to the mail. I could go down to Richmond and see her once – there was no disloyalty to Rich in that.

I had no intention of opening the little purse. I placed it under my pillow, which was why I refused to let Mrs. Klopton change the linen, much to her dismay. And sometimes during the morning, while lying under white sheets with peculiar floral patterns, my hidden cigarettes nearby and *Science and Health* on a table by my side, I would gently slide my hand under the pillow and touch the purse with reverence.

Around eleven, McKnight arrived. I heard his car pull up at the curb, followed closely by the sound of the front door slamming and his usual boisterous ascent up the stairs.

He brought a bottle and a box of cigarettes, suspecting I might have been deprived of stimulants.

"How did you sleep after keeping me up half the night?" he asked cheerfully.

I slid my hand around: the purse was well covered. "Have it now, or wait till I get the cork out?" he rattled on.

"I don't want anything," I protested. "And could you please stop being so overly cheerful, Richey?" He stopped whistling and stared at me.

"'I am saddest when I sing!'" he quoted solemnly. "It's just a reaction, Lollie. Yesterday the sky was low: I was searching for my best friend. Today, he lies before me, grumbling as usual. Yesterday, I thought the notes were burned. Today, I look forward to a thrilling chase, and with luck, we might catch them." His tone changed abruptly. "Yesterday, she was in Seal Harbor. Today, she is here."

"Here in Washington?" I asked casually.

"Yes. Staying for a week or two."

"Oh, I had a little hen and she had a wooden leg

And nearly every morning she used to lay an egg—"

"Will you stop that noise, Rich! Is it the real thing this time, I suppose?"

"She's the best little chicken that we have on the farm

And another little drink won't do us any harm—" he finished, twisting out the corkscrew. Then he came over and sat on the bed.

"Well," he said seriously, "since you drag it out of me, I think it might be. You're such a confirmed woman-hater that I wasn't sure how you'd take it."

"Nothing of the sort," I denied testily. "Just because a man reaches the age of thirty without making maudlin love to every—"

"I've taken to long country rides," he continued thoughtfully, ignoring my response, "and yesterday I almost hit a sheep; nearly went into the ditch. But there's a Providence that watches over fools and lovers, and right now, I know darn well that I'm one, and I have a sneaking suspicion I'm both."

"You are both," I said with disgust. "If you could be rational for a moment, could you tell me why that man Sullivan called me on the telephone yesterday morning?"

"Probably he hadn't discovered the Bronson notes yet – if we stick to your theory that the theft was secondary to the murder. Maybe he wanted his own clothes back or he wished to thank you for yours. Search me, I can't think of anything else."

The doctor entered at that moment. As I mentioned before, I have great respect for my doctor when I'm sick. He is a young man with a confident and good-natured demeanor. He looked past the bottle with remarkable skill and shook hands with McKnight until I could discreetly put the cigarettes under the bedclothes – he had prohibited tobacco. Then he sat down beside the bed and gently felt the bandages with hands as tender as a baby's.

"Looking good," he said. "How'd you sleep?"

"Okay, I guess," I replied. "I'd like to sit up, doctor."

"Nonsense. Rest while you can. I wish *I* could stay in bed for a day. I was up all night."

"Have a drink," McKnight offered, pushing the bottle over.

"Twins!" the doctor grinned.

"Have *two* drinks."

But the doctor declined. "I wouldn't even wear a champagne-colored tie during work hours," he explained. "By the way, I had another case from your accident, Mr. Blakeley, late yesterday afternoon. Under the tongue, please." He stuck a thermometer in my mouth.

I suddenly imagined the amateur detective's notebook, cheerful impertinence, and incriminating data coming to light. "A small man?" I asked, "gray hair…"

"Keep your mouth closed," the doctor said firmly. "No. A woman, with a fractured skull. Interesting case. Van Kirk called me in. Hemorrhage, right-sided paralysis, irregular pupils… all the works. Worked on her for two hours."

"Did she recover?" McKnight inquired, now looking at the doctor with newfound awe.

"She lifted her right arm before I left," the doctor concluded cheerily, "so the operation was a success, even if she should die."

"Good Lord," McKnight interjected, "and here I thought you were just an ordinary mortal like the rest of us! Let me touch you for luck. Was she pretty?"

"Yes, and young. Had a lot of bronze-colored hair. I truly hated to have to cut it."

McKnight and I exchanged glances. "Do you know her name, doctor?" I asked.

"No. The nurses said her clothes were from a tailor in Pittsburg."

"Is she conscious at all?"

"No, but she might be tomorrow … or in a week." He glanced at the thermometer, murmured something about a liquid diet, avoiding my eye – Mrs. Klopton was broiling a pork chop at the time – and left, humming cheerfully as he descended the stairs.

McKnight watched him wistfully. "Wow, I wish I had his constitution," he exclaimed. "No nerves or heart! He'd make an incredible chauffeur!"

But I was serious. "I have an idea," I said grimly, "that this murder matter will resurface, and your uncle will be in trouble if it does. If that woman is going to die, someone should be there to take her statement. She knows a lot, even if she's not the killer. Could you go to the telephone and call the hospital? Find out her name and whether she's conscious."

McKnight grumbled as he went. "I don't have much time," he said, checking his watch. "I'm meeting Mrs. West and Alison at one. You should meet them too, Lollie. You'd like the mother."

"Why not the daughter?" I asked, my hand touching the small gold purse under the pillow.

"Well," he said thoughtfully, "you've always been against the immaturity and romantic nonsense of young women…"

"I never said that!" I retorted angrily.

"*'There is more satisfaction to be had out of a good saddle horse!' You said that. 'More excitement out of a polo pony, and as for the eternal matrimonial chase, give me instead a good stubble, a fox, some decent hounds and a hunter, and I'll show you the real joys of the chase!'*" he quoted me.

"For Heaven's sake, go to the telephone. You're giving me a headache," I snapped. I don't know why, but I felt compelled to take out the gold purse and look at it. It was a foolish thing to do – call it impulse or sentimentality. I took it out, keeping an eye on the door, as Mrs. Klopton has a stealthy step. But the house was quiet. McKnight was downstairs, chatting with the telephone operator. I held up the purse and looked at it. It must have been unfastened, as in an instant, there was a scattering on the bed – a bit of money, a delicate handkerchief, a tiny booklet with powdery leaves, and a necklace. The necklace was one of those semi-barbaric pieces that women wear now, with a heavy pendant of gold chains and carved cameos, hanging from a delicate neck chain of the same metal. The necklace was broken, with three links pulled apart and the cameos loose and partly detached.

But it was the supporting chain that caught my eye, intriguing me with its sinister implication. Three inches of it had been snapped off, and as sure as I knew anything, that bit of chain the amateur detective had found, blood-stained and all, belonged right there.

I had no one to talk to about this, no one to tell me how absurd it was, and no one to slap me back to reality or to dismiss it as a mere coincidence.

Using my one useful hand, I hurriedly put the items back into the purse and buried it deep among the pillows. Then I lay back, feeling a cold sweat. What was Alison West's connection to this crime? Why did she stare so at the gun-metal cigarette case on the train? What alarmed her at the farm-house? What did she take back to the gate? Why did she wish she had not escaped from the wreck? And, most importantly, how did a part of her necklace end up torn off and covered in blood?

Downstairs, McKnight was still on the phone, entertaining himself with Mrs. Klopton while waiting for a response.

"Why did he come home in a gray suit when he left in a blue one?" he repeated her question. "Well, wrecks are strange things, Mrs. Klopton. The suit might have turned gray with fright. Or perhaps wrecks cause weird things to happen, like when lightning strikes. I once knew someone who got hit by lightning; he and the caddy took shelter under a tree. After the flash, they found my friend in the caddy's clothes, and the caddy in his. And as my friend was a large man and the caddy a small boy…" McKnight's story was cut short by the angry slam of the dining-room door. He had to wait for quite some time, and even his perpetual cheerfulness was fading when he finally got through to the hospital.

"Is Doctor Van Kirk there?" he asked. "Not there? Well, can you tell me about the patient Doctor Williams from Washington operated on last night? Oh, I'm glad to hear that. Is she conscious? Do you happen to know her name? Yes, I'll hold the line." There was a long pause, then McKnight's voice came again: "Hello? Yes. Thank you very much. Goodbye."

He came upstairs, bounding two steps at a time. "Listen," he said, bursting into the room, "there might be something to your theory after all. The woman's name – it might be just a coincidence, but it's interesting – her name is Sullivan."

"What did I tell you?" I said, sitting up suddenly in bed. "She's probably a sister of that scoundrel in lower seven, and she was afraid of what he might do."

"Well, I'll visit her soon. She's not conscious yet. Meanwhile, the only thing I can do is to keep an eye, through a detective, on the people who try to approach Bronson. We'll get the case extended, hoping the stolen notes will turn up eventually."

"This arm is a nuisance," I said, paying for my burst of activity with painful throbs. "There's so much to take care of, and here I am, all bandaged up, splinted, and utterly useless. It's truly frustrating."

"Don't forget that I'm here," said McKnight in a pompous tone. "And another thing, when you feel this way, just remember there are two worse places you could be: jail and…" He played an imaginary harp with a devout look.

But McKnight's lightheartedness didn't sit well with me that morning. I lay there, frowning in my helplessness. When I accidentally touched the little gold purse, it felt like it was burning my fingers. Richey, finding me unresponsive, left to keep his luncheon engagement with Alison West. As he clattered down the stairs, I wondered how Alison was holding up under the circumstances. Should I dare to return the purse? Would she hate me for having it? Or had I blown the importance of the necklace out of proportion, and in that case, had she had already forgotten about me?

But McKnight hadn't left after all. I heard him returning, his voice announcing his arrival, and I groaned with annoyance.

"Wake up!" he called. "Someone has sent you a huge bunch of flowers. Hold the box, Mrs. Klopton; I'm going out to get hit by a car."

I mustered some interest. My sister-in-law is very particular about such things; all the new babies in the family get silver rattles, and all the sick people receive flowers.

McKnight gathered an armful of roses and held them out to me. "I wonder who they're from?" he said, searching the box for a card. "There's no name… Wait, here's the card."

He held it up and read it with infuriating slowness.

"*'Best wishes for an early recovery. A companion in misfortune.'*

"Well, what do you know about that!" he exclaimed. "That's something you didn't tell me, Lollie."

"It wasn't worth mentioning," I lied, my heart pounding in my chest. She hadn't forgotten, after all.

McKnight took a bud and pinned it to his lapel. I must admit I wasn't particularly pleased about it. Those roses were meant for me. Richey left soon after, with an annoying grin at the flowers.

"Goodbye, Mr. woman-hater," he teased from the doorway.

So he wore one of the roses she had sent me to lunch with her, while I lay back among my pillows, trying to remind myself that it was his game anyway, and I wasn't even in the playing hand. I tried to remember that and to forget about the broken necklace under my head.

Chapter Thirteen
FADED ROSES

I was confined to the house for a week. During that time, I struggled with writing and discarding letters of thanks to Miss West while growling at the doctor. McKnight visited daily, but he seemed less cheerful than usual. Occasionally, he would glance at me as if he had something to say, but he kept it to himself. One day during that week, he went to Baltimore and visited the woman in the hospital there. From his description, I had little trouble recognizing her as the young woman who had been with the murdered man in Pittsburgh. However, she was still unconscious. An elderly aunt had appeared, a gaunt woman dressed in black, who sat around like a buzzard on a fence, as McKnight put it, weeping into a damp handkerchief.

On the last day of my confinement, McKnight dropped by to discuss a case coming up in court the next day and to play a game of double solitaire with me.

"Who won the baseball game?" I asked.

"We lost. Ask me something pleasant. Oh, by the way, Bronson is out today."

"I'm glad I'm not on his bond," I said gloomily. "He'll probably skip town."

"Not a chance," McKnight retorted, grabbing my ace. "He's no fool. Don't you think he knows you took those notes to Pittsburgh? It was all over the news. And he's well aware that you survived the wreck with a broken arm. What do we do next? The Commonwealth asks for a continuance of the case... Even a deaf man in the dark would know those notes are missing."

"Don't play so fast," I protested. "I only have one arm to your two. Who is tailing Bronson? Did you try to get Johnson?"

"I asked for him, but he had other work to do."

"The murder is a dead-end," I pondered. "So to speak... No, I'm serious. The wreck destroyed all the evidence. But I'm convinced those notes will surface soon, either offered to us or to Bronson. Johnson might be a scoundrel, but he's a good detective. He's persistent. What's he up to?"

McKnight put down his cards, walked to the window, and held the curtain back. His usual grin seemed a bit strained.

"To be honest, Lollie," he said, "for the past two days, Johnson has been watching a well-known Washington attorney named Lawrence Blakeley. He's across the street right now."

It took a moment for me to understand what he was implying.

"That's ridiculous," I asserted. "Why would they be following me? Go over and tell Johnson to leave, or I'll aim my revolver at him."

"You can tell him yourself," McKnight replied, leaning forward. "Hello, here's a visitor; a little man with a limp."

"I won't see him," I said firmly. "I've had enough of dealing with reporters."

We both listened to Mrs. Klopton's protesting voice in the hallway and the creaking of the stairs as she ascended heavily. In her hand, she held a torn piece of paper from a pocket account-book, with the name, "Mr. Wilson Budd Hotchkiss. Important business."

"Oh well, show him in," I said resignedly. "You should put those cards away, Richey. I have a feeling it's the rector from the nearby church."

But when the door opened and a strangely alert little man entered, adjusting his glasses with nervous fingers, my face must have revealed my dismay: It was the amateur detective from the Ontario!

I greeted him without enthusiasm, knowing that he was the one survivor of the wrecked car who could potentially harm me. There was little hope that he had forgotten any of the incriminating details. In fact, he held in his hand the very notebook that contained them.

His manner was controlled, but it was clear he was highly excited. I introduced him to McKnight, who has the imagination I lack, and who quickly sized him up.

"I only found out yesterday that you had been... saved," the little man said rapidly. "A terrible accident... unspeakable. I dream about it all night and think about it all day. Broken arm?"

"No, he just wears the splint to be different from other people," McKnight quipped lazily. I glared at him, knowing that antagonizing the little man wouldn't help.

"Yes, a fractured humerus, which isn't as funny as it sounds."

"Humerus… humorous! Not bad," he chuckled. "I must say you're keeping up your spirits pretty well, considering everything."

"You seem to have escaped injury," I replied. He was fumbling for something in his pockets.

"Yes, I escaped," he answered absentmindedly. "A remarkable thing, too. I have no doubt I would have broken my neck, but I landed on… you'll never guess what! I landed headfirst on the very pillow that was under inspection at the time of the wreck. Do you remember, don't you? Where did I put that package?"

After a search, he found it and opened it on the table, dramatically displaying a rectangular piece of muslin and a similar patch of striped ticking.

"Do you recognize it?" he said. "The stains, you see, and the hole made by the dagger. I tried to take the whole pillow, but they thought I was stealing it and forced me to give it up."

Richey touched the pieces cautiously. "By George," he exclaimed, "and you carry that around in your pocket! What if you mistake it for your handkerchief?"

But Mr. Hotchkiss was not paying attention. He stood bent slightly forward, leaning over the table, and fixed his ferret-like eyes on me.

"Have you seen the evening papers, Mr. Blakeley?" he inquired.

I looked over to where the unopened newspapers lay and shook my head.

"Then I have an unpleasant task ahead," he said with evident satisfaction. "You probably thought the matter of Harrington's death was closed after the wreck. I did too. As far as I was concerned, I intended to leave it that way. There were no other survivors, at least none that I knew of, and despite the circumstances, there were several points in your favor."

"Thank you very much," I interjected with a sarcasm that went over his head.

"I verified your identity, for instance, as soon as I recovered from the shock. Also, I inquired with your tailor and found out that you always wore dark clothing."

McKnight stepped forward threateningly. "Who are you, anyway?" he demanded. "And why is this any of your business?"

Mr. Hotchkiss remained entirely composed. "I have a minor role here," he said, reaching for a visiting card. "I am a very small cog in the government's machinery, sir."

McKnight muttered something about certain undesirable designs against said cog and grumbled as he retreated to the window. Our visitor energetically opened the newspaper. "Here it is. Listen." He read quickly aloud:

"The Pittsburg police have sent two detectives to Baltimore to investigate the survivors of the ill-fated Washington Flier. It has come to light that Simon Harrington, the Wood Street merchant from that city, was not killed in the wreck but was actually murdered in his berth the night before the accident. Shortly before the collision, John Flanders, the conductor of the Flier, sent this telegram to the chief of police:

'Body of Simon Harrington found stabbed in his berth, lower ten, Ontario, at six-thirty this morning. JOHN FLANDERS, Conductor.'

It is hoped that the survivors of the wrecked car Ontario will come forward to provide information about the discovery of the crime.

Mr. John Gilmore, head of the steel company for which Mr. Harrington was a purchasing agent, has expressed his intention to thoroughly investigate the matter.

"So you see," Hotchkiss concluded, "there's trouble brewing. You and I are the only survivors of that unfortunate car."

I didn't correct him, but I knew of at least two others: Alison West and the woman we had left by the road that morning, muttering incoherently with her black hair falling over her pale face.

"Unless we can find the man who occupied lower seven," I suggested.

"I've already tried and failed. Even if we find him, it wouldn't necessarily clear you unless we can establish some connection between him and the murdered man. But it's the only lead I see. I've learned this much," Hotchkiss concluded, "berth lower seven was reserved from Cresson."

Cresson! Where Alison West and Mrs. Curtis had boarded the train!

McKnight stepped forward and extended his hand. "Mr. Hotchkiss," he said, "I apologize if I've been offensive. When you first came in, I thought you were against us. If you're willing to put those interesting relics aside, I'd be pleased to have you join me for dinner at the Incubator." (The Incubator was his name for his bachelor apartment.) "Compared to Johnson, you're the real deal."

Hotchkiss accepted the invitation, and they left together. From my window, I watched them get into McKnight's car. It was raining, and the Cannonball skidded at the corner. Across the street, my detective, Johnson, observed them with his crooked smile. As he turned up his collar, he noticed me and tipped his hat.

I left the window and sat down in the growing dusk, musing about the new information. So the occupant of lower seven had boarded at Cresson, likely with Alison West and her companion. There was someone she cared about enough to protect. Annoyed, I went to the door and called for Mrs. Klopton.

"You can dispose of those roses," I said, without looking at her. "They are completely wilted."

"They've been wilted for three days," she retorted spitefully. "Euphemia said you threatened to fire her if she touched them."

Chapter Fourteen
THE TRAP-DOOR

A week after the wreck, by Sunday evening, my inaction was driving me crazy. Every time I saw Johnson across the street or lurking nearby, it just annoyed me even more. It was on that day that things began to become clearer, and it felt like all events were revolving around me, and I couldn't escape it.

That evening, I had a solitary dinner, feeling anything but cheerful. The polo match from the day before had been a disaster – I had lent a pony, which is always a bad idea, and she ended up hurting her shoulder and contributing to our team's loss. To top it off, there was no one else in town, the temperature was a scorching ninety degrees and rising, and my left hand kept cramping painfully under its bandage.

Mrs. Klopton, ever the caring figure, tried to cheer me up as she served my meal. "The paper says it's getting warmer," she ventured. "The thermometer is already at ninety-two."

I sighed, putting down my cup of coffee. "And this coffee feels like it's two hundred and fifty degrees," I remarked. "By the way, where's Euphemia? I haven't seen her around or heard her break anything today."

With a grave tone, Mrs. Klopton informed me: "Euphemia is in bed."

"What's the matter with her?" I inquired idly.

"Frightened out of her wits," Mrs. Klopton said in a stage whisper. "She's had three hot water bottles and she hasn't done a thing all day but moan."

"She oughtn't to take hot water bottles," I said in my severest tone. "One would make me moan. You need not wait, I'll ring if I need anything."

Mrs. Klopton, indignant yet steadfast, made her way to the door. Before leaving, she turned to face me and declared, "I just hope you won't regret ignoring this situation, Mr. Lawrence. I'm going to have the police keep an eye on that house next door."

I had half a mind to tell her that both our house and the neighbor's were already under police surveillance. However, my fondness for Mrs. Klopton held me back. Despite how I made her life difficult, I genuinely liked her.

She continued, "Last night, when the paper mentioned that it was going to storm, I sent Euphemia to the roof to bring in the rugs. Eliza had slipped out, despite it being her evening to work. Euphemia went up to the roof around eleven o'clock, and soon after, I heard her running downstairs, crying. When she reached my room, she simply collapsed on the floor. She said there was a black figure sitting on the parapet of the empty house next door, waving long black arms and hissing at her like a cat."

I had finished my dinner and was lighting a cigarette. I casually remarked, "If there was anyone up there, which I doubt, maybe they just sneezed. But don't worry, I'll check the roof tonight before going to bed. As for Euphemia, she always has some kind of attack when Eliza slips out unexpectedly and she has to work in her place."

Later that night, I made a quick examination of the window locks and explored parts of the house I hadn't seen since I bought it. The roof, accessible only by a ladder and a trap-door, was a bit tricky to reach with my injured arm. Still, I managed to get up there and enjoyed the coolness of the night while sitting on the brick parapet, smoking my last cigarette. The roof of the empty house was connected to mine along the back wing, but the trap-door across the low dividing wall was securely bolted from below. Convinced that there was nothing unusual, I assured Mrs. Klopton of the same. However, I didn't mention that I had left the trap-door open to test if it would improve the house's temperature. I went to bed around midnight, turning on the night lamp and picking up a random volume of Shaw's work (*Arms and the Man*) to read myself to sleep. I have no apologies to make for what occurred that night, and not even an explanation that I am sure of. I did a foolish thing under impulse, and I haven't been sorry.

Around two in the morning, the doorbell rang twice, snapping me awake. As the maids and Mrs. Klopton usually lock themselves beyond reach of the bell at night, I put on a dressing-gown. The bell rang again while I made my way downstairs, where I lit the hall light and opened the door. To my surprise, it was Johnson, his bald head gleaming under the light, and a twisted smile on his crooked mouth.

"Good Heavens, man," I snapped irritably. "Don't you ever go home and sleep?"

He entered the entrance hall and switched off the light. Our conversation was terse and tense.

"Do you have a key to the empty house next door?" he demanded. "Someone's in there, and the latch is stuck."

"The houses are identical. The key to this door might fit. Did you see anyone enter?"

"No, but there's a light moving from room to room. I saw something similar last night, and I've been keeping watch. The patrolman reported strange happenings there about a week ago."

"A light?" I exclaimed. "Do you mean that you…"

"Very likely," he replied grimly. "Do you have a revolver?"

"I've got all sorts in the gun rack," I answered, going into the den and returning with a Smith and Wesson. "I'm not much use with this arm, but I'll do what I can. The servants here have been feeling uneasy."

Johnson devised a plan. He suggested that, because of my familiarity with the roof, I should go up there and block any escape attempts in that direction. "Robison, the patrolman on the beat, is outside," he said. "He'll watch below, and you'll be above, while I search the house. Let's be as quiet as possible."

The situation rather amused me. I dressed quickly and carefully ascended the stairs, the revolver ready in my pocket, my hand gripping the rail. At the base of the ladder, I stopped and looked up at the gray sky sprinkled with stars. It occurred to me that with only one good hand holding the ladder, I wasn't well-positioned to defend myself. I was about to raise my vulnerable body into a danger I couldn't see. I must admit those seconds climbing the ladder were among the most unpleasant moments of my life.

Nonetheless, I reached the top without incident. After the darkness of the house below, my eyes adjusted, and I could see fairly well. However, there was nothing suspicious in sight. The rooftops, separated by a two-foot brick wall, spread out around me, interrupted only by the occasional chimney. I moved quietly to the trap of the suspected house. It was closed, and I thought I could hear Johnson's heavy footsteps ascending. Then even that sound disappeared. A nearby clock struck three while I stood waiting. It was then that I checked my revolver for the first time, only to discover that it was empty!

Until that moment, I had maintained my skepticism and displayed the bravado of a man roused from his sleep to search for burglars, armed only with a gun. But as I discovered my empty revolver, my confidence turned into the fear of a man standing atop an erupting volcano. My eyes were fixed on the trap-door beneath me, which I had examined and confirmed was bolted earlier. Now, to my astonishment, it seemed to be raising slightly. My heart raced, and I couldn't help but imagine the worst. With just one good arm against an intruder with two, I felt a sense of impending danger, and my knees trembled with fear.

Johnson's footsteps were audible from a distance below, and the trap-door, raised by about two inches, remained motionless. There was no sound coming from beneath it, except for a moment when I thought I heard a few labored breaths, which might have been my own.

Then, out of nowhere, a hand appeared, clutching the frame of the trap-door. Acting on instinct, I did the only thing I could think of – I placed my foot on the hand. To my surprise, there was no sound from below. I quickly kneeled and grabbed the wrist above the hand. Having something tangible to confront, my composure returned.

"Stay still, or I'll stand on the trap and break your arm," I warned, using whatever threat I could muster. Shooting or fighting wasn't an option for me in that moment. "Johnson!" I called out.

What followed haunted me for weeks, and even now, the memory sends shivers down my spine. The hand felt icy cold and strangely lifeless. I could barely feel a faint pulse in the wrist. Strangely slender, the hand seemed almost unreal. I held it up to the starlight for a closer look… and then I let it drop.

"Good Lord," I mumbled, still kneeling and staring at the spot where the hand had been. It had vanished, and all I heard was a soft rustling below, followed by silence.

In the dim starlight, I examined a long scratch on my own palm, still trying to comprehend what had just happened. "A woman!" I blurted out, stunned by the bizarre turn of events. "Unbelievable, it was a woman!"

Meanwhile, Johnson was busy striking matches below and cursing softly, "How the devil do you get to the roof? I think I've broken my nose."

He eventually located the ladder and stood below, looking up at me. "Well, I suppose you haven't seen him?" he asked. "This house has enough hidden nooks to conceal a wagon full of thieves." He struck another match. "Hello, here's another door!"

I heard his footsteps receding, likely indicating he was on a rear staircase. After about ten minutes, he returned, this time with the policeman.

"He's gone, alright," Johnson said with regret. "If you'd been doing your job, Robison, you would have watched the back door."

"I'm not capable of being in two places at once," Robison retorted, grumpy.

"Well," I chimed in, trying to sound cheerful, "if you're done with this eventful adventure and can descend my ladder without causing my housekeeper to trigger the burglar alarm, I have some excellent Monongahela whisky… what do you say?"

Without hesitation, they crossed the roof and joined me. Once they were away from the house, I felt a sense of relief. In the den, I fulfilled my promise of a drink. Johnson seemed to be intrigued by my collection of guns, eyeing them like a connoisseur. Even as he was about to leave, he couldn't resist casting a longing glance back at the firearms.

"Ever served in the army?" he asked.

"No," I replied with a bitterness he picked up on but failed to understand. "I'm a chocolate cream soldier. You probably don't read Shaw, do you, Johnson?"

"Never heard of him," the detective responded indifferently. "Well, good night, Mr. Blakeley. Thanks for your cooperation." He paused at the door and cleared his throat.

"I hope you understand, Mr. Blakeley," he said awkwardly, "that this, uh, surveillance is all part of the job. I don't like it, but it's my duty. Every man has his duty, sir."

"Someday, when you're feeling more forthcoming, Johnson," I replied, "maybe you can explain why I'm being watched in the first place."

Chapter Fifteen
AT THE VAUDEVILLE

- NOTES -

THE CINEMATOGRAPH – A very short silent film clip. At the beginning of the 1900s, film was still in its infancy, and technological limitations allowed movies to last only about thirty seconds. This of course, coupled with the lack of sound, limited the ability of a movie to actually tell a story. Early films were true novelties, and they were often shown at vaudeville shows, the most popular form of entertainment in the first decade of 1900. Vaudeville shows contained nine to twelve acts, showcasing comedy, stunts, dramatic skits, and singing. Vaudeville acts toured from city to city, and the best performers of the most famous acts became real stars. In this chapter of The Man in Lower Ten, *our protagonists go to the theater to enjoy a vaudeville show and they see a short movie clip – a Cinematograph – that will be important to the development of the story.*

On Monday, I headed out for the first time, skipping the office to take a walk. I hoped the fresh air and exercise would chase away my emotional turmoil. McKnight wanted a long car ride, but I declined.

"Why not?" he pouted. "I can't walk. Haven't walked two blocks in years. Cars have rendered legs mere ornaments, and some not even that. We could have Johnson tailing us at two bucks an hour!"

"He can tail us just fine at two miles an hour," I replied. "But what baffles me, McKnight, is why I'm being watched. How did the police know *I* was accused of that thing?"

"The girl who sent the flowers, she won't talk, will she?"

"No. Actually, I didn't mention it was a girl." I winced while trying to put on my coat with my splinted arm. "Either way, she didn't talk," I insisted, and McKnight chuckled.

It had rained in the early morning, and Mrs. Klopton forecasted more rain. So convinced was she, I had to take the umbrella she offered. "Don't worry," I said. "We can leave it next door. I've got a story for you, Richey, and it needs the right ambiance."

McKnight was puzzled but obediently followed me to the kitchen entrance of the vacant house. As I had anticipated, it was unlocked. While climbing to the upper floor, I recounted the events of the previous night.

"It's the best thing I've heard," McKnight said, gazing at the ladder and trapdoor. "What a funny sketch it would make! But you probably shouldn't have stepped on her hand. That's not kosher in proper circles."

I turned to him impatiently. "You're not getting the whole picture, Richey!" I exclaimed. "What if I told you it was a *lady's* hand? Covered in rings."

"A lady!" he echoed. "Well, I'd say that's quite a compromising situation. The less said, the better. Look, Lawrence, I think you dreamt it. You've been cooped up in the house too much. I take back what I said; you do need exercise."

"She likely escaped through this door," I said, as calmly as I could. "Probably down the back stairs. We might as well head down that way."

"Following the usual playbook, we'd find a glove around here," he remarked as we descended. But he was more shaken than he let on. He scrutinized the dusty steps carefully, and when a piece of loose plaster fell just behind him, he jumped like a frightened cat.

"What I can't figure out is why you let her go," he said, pausing and looking puzzled. "You're not usually so impractical."

"Once we're out in the countryside, Richey," I said seriously, "I'll share another tale with you. And if you don't call me a fool and a coward after hearing it, then you're no true friend of mine."

We stumbled down the dimly lit staircase and entered the dark kitchen. The house had that musty odor of unused buildings. Even on that warm September morning, it felt damp and cold. As we stepped into the sunlight, McKnight shivered.

"Now that we're out," he commented, "I'll confess that I've been there before. Remember the night you left and the face in the window?"

"When you mention it… yes."

"Well, that incident piqued my curiosity," he continued as we walked up the street, "so I went back. The front door was unlocked, and I explored every room. I was Mrs. Klopton's ghost, carrying a light and climbing."

"Did you discover anything?"

"Only a clean spot rubbed on the window across from your dressing room. Perfect view of a messy interior. If that house ever gets occupied, you might want to put stained glass in that window of yours."

As we turned the corner, I glanced behind us. Johnson was trailing us about half a block away. He stopped and leisurely lit a cigar when he noticed me, but he managed to catch the same streetcar as us, standing inconspicuously on the rear platform. He seemed weary, and absent-mindedly paid our fares, much to McKnight's amusement.

"We'll give him a good chase," McKnight declared as the car headed towards the countryside. "Conductor, drop us off at the muddiest lane you can find."

By one o'clock, after a six-mile stroll, we entered a small rural inn. We hadn't seen Johnson for half an hour. He was a quarter-mile behind us at that point, and falling behind quickly. By the time we finished our lunch, he stumbled into the inn. He had one boot under his arm, and his appearance was a mess. Covered in mud, sweat-streaked, limping along. He chose a table near us and ordered a Scotch. Besides a nod, he paid us no mind.

"I'm just getting my second wind," McKnight said. "How are you holding up, Mr. Johnson? A few more miles and we'll all be ready for dinner."

Johnson put his glass down without a word.

The truth was, I felt a lot like Johnson. A week of inactivity had left me out of shape, and I was quite worn out. McKnight, full of energy and enthusiasm, concocted a peculiar mixture from the bar's offerings and sent it over to the detective, who declined it.

"I can't stand those types," McKnight grumbled. "They act like you're trying to poison their dog if you offer him a bone."

As we made our way back to the streetcar stop, Johnson trailing behind us like a ragged kite's tail, I felt better. I had shared the story of the three hours following the accident with McKnight, though I hadn't mentioned the girl's name; I had given her my word of secrecy.

However, I spilled all the other details to him. It felt good to have a fresh perspective on it all; I had been over thinking the incident at the farmhouse and the necklace in the gold purse to the point of confusion.

He had shown interest, but was inclined to be amused, until I reached the part about the broken chain. Then he let out a low whistle. "But there are countless gold chains made every year," he remarked. "Why on earth do you think that the—um—dirty piece came from that necklace?"

I glanced around, seeing Johnson lagging behind, using a stick to scrape mud off his shoes.

"I've got the shorter end of the chain in the sealskin bag," I reminded him. "Couldn't sleep this morning, so I decided to settle it once and for all. The uncertainty was driving me mad. And there's no doubt about it, Rich. It's the same chain."

We walked in silence until we caught the streetcar back to town.

"Well," he finally said, "you know the girl, of course. You're acquainted with her, and I'm not. But if you're fond of her – and I suspect you're quite taken, my friend – I wouldn't give a damn about the chain in the gold purse. It's just one of those little coincidences that trip people up now and then. And as for last night… If she's the kind of girl you describe, and you believe she had anything to do with that, then you're a bit muddled. Mark my words, the lady from the vacant house last week is the same one from last night. And yet your train companion was in Altoona at that time."

Just before we got off the streetcar, I circled back to the subject again. It never strayed far from my thoughts. "Regarding the young lady from the train, Rich," I said with a carefully crafted casual tone, "I don't want you to misconstrue. I'm not very likely to cross paths with her again, but even if I do, I suspect she's already taken, or nearly so."

He didn't respond, merely standing on the pavement, gazing up at me with his characteristic bemused smile. "Love is like the measles," he quipped. "The older you catch it, the harder it hits."

Johnson didn't make an appearance for the rest of the day. Instead, a small man in a raincoat took his place.

The following morning, I went to the office, raincoat still in tow. I had a brief meeting with Miller, the district attorney, at eleven. Bronson was being watched, he informed me, and any attempt to sell the notes to him would likely lead to their recovery. Meanwhile, as I was aware, the Commonwealth had continued the case, hoping for such an outcome.

By noon, I had left the office and arranged for a veterinarian to examine Candida, the injured pony. My initial tasks for the day were completed by one o'clock, leaving me with a scorching afternoon ahead. McKnight, always eager to escape the routine, proposed going to a vaudeville show, and out of sheer boredom, I agreed. Unable to ride, drive, or play golf, my own company was becoming insufferable.

"Coolest spot in town these days," he exclaimed. "Electric fans, breezy tunes, light costumes. And there's Johnson trailing behind…the coldest proposition in Washington."

He solemnly bought three tickets, handing one over to the detective, and we entered. Having lived a regular, busy life, afternoon theater is akin to having ice cream for breakfast.

Onstage, a rather plump lady in short pink skirts, her smile resembling – as McKnight put it – a slash in a roll of butter, was singing in a nasal tone, punctuating each verse with a laborious kick. Johnson, a couple of rows ahead, dozed off.

McKnight nudged me. "Check out the first box on the right," he whispered theatrically. "I want you to come over after this act."

It was my first sight of her since I left her in that cab in Baltimore. Outwardly, I probably appeared composed, as no one turned to stare, but every fiber of my being reacted to her presence. Leaning forward, lips slightly parted, she was captivated by the Japanese magician who had taken over the stage. Compared to the disheveled lady at the farmhouse, she looked radiant. For that initial moment, sheer joy overwhelmed me at the sight of her, but McKnight's touch on my arm snapped me back to reality.

"Let's go meet them," he urged. "That's Miss West's cousin, Mrs. Dallas."

But I wouldn't go. After he left, I sat alone, acutely aware of being watched and pointed at from the box. The dreadful Japanese act gave way to an even worse performance by trained dogs.

"How many marriage proposals will the lady in the box receive?" The dog stopped smartly at "none" and then revealed a card that read "eight." The crowd erupted in laughter. "Fools," I muttered.

After a while, I glanced over. Mrs. Dallas conversed with McKnight, but *her* gaze was fixed directly on me. She appeared flushed yet composed, and she didn't nod or acknowledge me. I fumbled for my hat, but then noticed they were leaving, so I stayed put. McKnight returned with an air of triumph.

"I've got plans for you," he announced. "Mrs. Dallas invited me and you to dinner tonight, and I assured her you'd practically fall over yourself to accept. You're asked to bring your fractured arm and any other mementos from the accident."

"I won't do any such thing," I protested, wrestling with my inclination. "I can't even tie my own necktie, and I need help cutting my food."

"Relax," he replied nonchalantly. "I'll send Stogie over to help you get ready, and Mrs. Dallas knows all about your arm. I told her."

(Stogie is his Japanese assistant.)

The Cinematograph was wrapping up the show. The theater was dimmed, and the music ceased, as it does at the circus just before someone risks their neck for a fee in the "Dip of Death" or a hundred-foot dive. Then, with a jolt, I saw the announcement on the white screen

THE NEXT PICTURE
CAPTURES THE ILL-FATED WASHINGTON FLIER,
SHORTLY BEFORE THE WRECK OCCURRED ON THAT
FATAL MORNING OF SEPTEMBER TENTH.
MERELY TWO MILES AHEAD, IT MET NEAR TOTAL
ANNIHILATION.

A wave of queasiness akin to the sensations from the crash returned. Around me, people leaned forward, faces taut with tension. Then the text disappeared, replaced by a wide, level expanse of tracks, even the crushed stones between the ties visible. In the distance, shrouded in smoke, a small object raced toward us, growing larger as it approached.

Suddenly, it was upon us, huge, sporting massive wheels and an enormous tender. The engine swerved to the side, seemingly barely avoiding our destruction, revealing a glimpse of a hunched fireman and a soot-covered engineer. The long train of sleepers trailed behind. A porter in a white coat waved from a front vestibule. The rest of the cars seemed still wrapped in slumber. With mixed emotions, I watched my own carriage, Ontario, speed by. And then, rising to my feet, I clutched McKnight's shoulder.

On the bottom step of the final car, one foot dangling, stood a man. His black derby hat was firmly pulled down to prevent it from being whisked away by the wind, and his coat fluttered in the breeze. He swung outward from the car, his free hand clutching a small valise, every muscle primed for a leap.

"Good Lord, that's my man!" I exclaimed hoarsely, as the audience erupted in applause. McKnight partially rose; Johnson, seated ahead of us, stifled a yawn and turned to scrutinize me. I slumped back into my seat, attempting to contain my excitement. "The man on the last platform of the train," I muttered. "He was just about to jump; I'd bet my life that was my bag."

"Did you see his face?" McKnight inquired softly. "Would you recognize him if you saw him again?"

"No. His hat was pulled low, and he was looking down. I'm going to investigate where that scene was filmed. They say two miles, but it could have been much farther."

The audience, occupied with their belongings, had not taken note. Mrs. Dallas and Alison West had departed. In front of us, Johnson dropped his hat and bent to retrieve it.

"This way," I gestured to McKnight, and we slipped into the narrow passage behind the boxes. At its end, a door led to the backstage area, and as we confidently entered, I locked the door behind us.

The final set was being dismantled, and no one paid us any attention. Fortunately, they appeared equally indifferent to the pounding at the door I had locked, which I assumed indicated Johnson's presence.

"I think we've thwarted his intrusion," McKnight chuckled.

Stagehands scurried in all directions; fragments of the last drawing-room's side wall menaced us; a switchboard nearby emitted a whistling sound akin to a teapot. Everywhere we stepped, we got in someone's way. Finally reaching the other side, we faced a man in his undershirt who, through a barrage of curses, seemed to be directing the chaos.

"Well?" he demanded, pivoting toward us. "What can I do for you?"

"I'd like to inquire," I began, "whether you have any knowledge about the location of the last shot in the film."

"Broken board—picnickers—lake?"

"No, the Washington Flier," I clarified.

He glanced at my bandaged arm.

"The announcement mentions two miles," McKnight interjected, "but we're curious about whether that's measured in railroad miles, automobile miles, or perhaps some unique unit like 'policeman miles.'"

"I'm sorry I can't provide that information," he replied, in a more courteous tone. "We obtain those pictures through contracts. We don't handle the filming ourselves."

"Where can we find the company's offices?"

"In New York." He approached a crew member and grabbed his shoulder. "What on earth are you doing with that gold chair in a kitchen setting? Take that piece of pink plush over there and toss it on a soapbox, unless you have a kitchen chair available."

The extent of the shock hit me all at once. I sank into a chair and wiped my forehead. The unexpected sight of Alison West, followed closely by the revelation from the film, had left me weak and unsettled. McKnight checked his watch.

"He says the movie folks have an office downtown. If we go now, we can make it."

So, he hailed a cab, and we sped off. There was no sign of the detective. "Honestly," Richey remarked, "I feel a bit lonesome without him."

The staff at the downtown movie company office was quite helpful. They informed us that the image had been captured at M——, merely two miles beyond the wreckage site. It wasn't much, but it was a starting point.

I decided not to return home but to send McKnight's Japanese assistant for my attire and get dressed at McKnight's flat, the Incubator. I was resolved to conduct my next day's investigations without Johnson's presence. Meanwhile, I would see *Her* that evening, perhaps for the final time.

I gave Stogie a note for Mrs. Klopton and along with my dinner clothes, the gold purse arrived, carefully wrapped in tissue paper.

Chapter Sixteen
THE SHADOW OF A GIRL

ARC LIGHT – An arc light, or arc lamp, is a lamp providing illumination by an electric arc. It was the first electric light to be widely used, starting in the 1870s, for the lighting of streets and large buildings. In the early 20th century, it was superseded by the incandescent light, the same technology used in ordinary light bulbs until they, in turn were replaces by LEDs. When this novel takes place, in 1909, electric arc lighting was still in wide use for public lighting.

The dinner at the Dallas house is a blur. Mr. Dallas was a Fish Commission guy and talked fish eggs as we ate caviar. I remember him saying that he wanted to move factories away from river-banks, claiming the fish were being bothered by the smoke or the noise or the stuff they were putting into the water. I can't really remember the details.

Mrs. Dallas was there, I assume. I do remember there was a woman in yellow who loosened my clams for me. But the one thing I do know for sure is that there was a radiant young woman in white sitting across from me, glowing in a haze of candlelight and framed by orchids. She was as brilliant as I was dull and never once glanced in my direction.

When the dinner had progressed from salmon to roast – and the conversation had done the same, from fish to scandal – Yellow Gown turned to me. "We've been good, right, Mr. Blakeley? No 'wreck' talk at all. I'm sure you must feel like the survivor of Waterloo, or something of the sort."

"Wreck talk?" I said, glancing at her. "Sorry to disappoint, but I recall nothing."

"Forgetfulness is a blessing," Miss West chimed in pointedly from her seat across the table. They were the first words she had spoken to me, and my courage surged.

"I do remember some things," I said, "I recall a beautiful girl trying to wake me, she said I'd been on fire twice."

"Come on, there's going to be more to this," Yellow Gown interjected, clearly intrigued. "That's seriously the most teasing tidbit I've ever heard." Miss West was now looking daggers at me.

"That's pretty much the end of it," I replied lamely. "We went our separate ways. If she even remembers me, it's probably as some guy who faints at the drop of a hat."

"See, I told you!" she exclaimed, triumphant. "He fainted, did you catch that? When it was all over! He's not telling the whole story."

By then, I thoroughly regretted bringing up the girl. But McKnight picked up the thread and ran with it.

"Blakeley's like a volcano," he remarked. "Doesn't erupt until he's boiling over. And you know what? Despite his lack of words about the Lady of the Wreck, I'm convinced he's head over heels for her. Bet my bottom dollar on it. He thinks he's keeping it under wraps, but trust me, it's written all over his face. Just look at him!"

I squirmed uncomfortably, avoiding the gaze of the girl across from me. I wanted to throttle McKnight.

"Not fair," I retorted as calmly as possible. "I've got my fingers crossed here; it's five against one."

"And let's not forget there was a murder on that train," chimed in Yellow Gown. "Talk about a crescendo of horrors, right? So, Mr. Blakeley, what happened to the murdered man?"

McKnight wisely jumped in to rescue me from answering. "They say when good Pittsburghers die, they go to Atlantic City," he quipped. "So, safe to say the guy *didn't* end up at the beach."

Finally, the meal wrapped up, and in the drawing-room, we seemed to be a burden for our hostess.

"Finding people for bridge in September is a struggle," she lamented. "Absolutely no one's around. Six is a dreadful number."

"Works great for poker though," her husband suggested.

However, the situation resolved itself. I was hopeless, save as a dummy. Miss West declared it too hot for cards and went to the balcony overlooking the Mall. With evident relief, Mrs. Dallas had the card table set up, and I was faced with the moment I'd been dreading and anticipating for a week.

Now that it was here, it was trickier than I'd imagined. I can't confirm if there was a moon, but there was the city's version of it, the arc light. It cast the shadow of the balcony railing's in long, black bars on her white dress. As it swung, her face alternated between light and shadow. I positioned a chair close to watch her intently.

"Do you realize," I began, "that you're far more impressive tonight, in that dress, than the last time I saw you?"

The light swung on her face; she faintly smiled. "The hat with the green ribbons!" she reminisced. "I almost forgot about that."

"I haven't forgotten… anything." I stopped myself abruptly. This wasn't showing much loyalty to Richey. His voice drifted in through the window, and maybe I was mistaken, but it seemed like she lifted her head to listen.

"He's a sweetheart, isn't he?" Alison remarked unexpectedly. "No matter how low I'm feeling, Richey always lifts my spirits."

"He's more than that," I responded warmly. "He's the most honorable guy I know. If he wasn't so dedicated to that, he could have a bright future. He even suggested we put 'Blakeley and McKnight, P. B. H.' on our office doors, which stands for Poor But Honest."

From my modest circumstances to the affluence of the girl beside me was a quick mental jump. From her wealth to the grandfather who had made it possible was another leap.

"Do you know that I'd just been to Pittsburgh to see your grandfather when I first met you?" I mentioned.

"You?" she appeared surprised.

"Yes. And remember the alligator bag that I told you was swapped for the one you cut off my arm?" She nodded, curious. "Well, in that bag were the forged Andy Bronson notes, along with Mr. Gilmore's sworn statement confirming their forgery."

She was on her feet in an instant. "In that bag!" she exclaimed. "Oh, why didn't you tell me this earlier? It's so absurd, so… so bleak. I could have…" she halted abruptly and settled back down. "I don't know if I'm sorry about it, after all," she spoke after a pause. "Mr. Bronson was a friend of my father's. I suppose it was a setback for you, losing those papers?"

"Well, it definitely wasn't a positive turn of events," I admitted. "And since we're discussing lost items, do you remember… do you know that I still have your gold purse?"

She didn't respond right away. The shadow of a column crossed her face, but I had a feeling she was studying me. "You have it!" Her voice was almost a whisper.

"I found it on the streetcar," I said, feigning a cheerfulness I wasn't feeling. "Looks like quite the luxurious little purse."

Why didn't she mention the necklace? Just a casual word could bring back my sanity!

"You!" she repeated, horrified. Then I revealed the purse, extending it on my open palm. "I probably should've returned it to you earlier, but, as you know, I've been laid up since the accident."

We both saw McKnight at the same moment. He pulled the curtains aside, spotting us. The whole scene was crystal clear: the gold purse, her hand reaching out, my attitude. It lasted just a moment before he stepped out and leaned against the balcony railing.

"They're giving me a hard time in there," he said casually. "So, I decided to escape. I guess they call it bridge because it drives so many people to the brink of one."

The heat soon dispersed the card players, and they joined us outside for the evening breeze. I never had a chance to talk to Alison privately again.

I returned to the Incubator for the night. Our journey back was mostly silent; an unfamiliar tension hung between us. It was too early for sleep, so we sat in the living room, smoking and attempting to engage in small talk. Eventually, even that petered out, leaving us in silence. It was McKnight who eventually addressed the elephant in the room.

"So, she wasn't in Seal Harbor at all," he remarked.

"No," I confirmed.

"Do you know where she was, Lollie?"

"Somewhere near Cresson."

"And that was the purse — her purse — with the broken necklace inside?"

"Yes, that's right. You see, Rich, I hope you understand that, having given her my word, I couldn't divulge the details to you?"

"I understand more than you might think," he responded, without bitterness.

We sat in silence, puffing on our cigarettes. Then Richey stood up and stretched. "I'm calling it a night, buddy," he declared. "Need any help with that injured arm of yours?"

"No, I'm good," I replied.

I heard him enter his room and lock the door. It was a tough moment for me. The first shadow between us, the shadow of a girl.

Chapter Seventeen
AT THE FARM-HOUSE AGAIN

McKnight is always an early bird, but that morning he appeared when it was quite late. Perhaps he had not slept well, like me. He seemed fairly cheerful, though, and ate a heartier breakfast than I did.

By one o'clock, we reached Baltimore, then waited thirty minutes for a local heading to M——, the station near where the movie picture was taken.

As we passed the wreckage site, curiosity filled McKnight, while I was overwhelmed by a sickening horror. There was the little farmhouse in the fields where Alison West and I planned to get coffee. Winding away from the tracks, was the lane, flanked by maple trees, where we had rested, and where I had – now unbelievably presumptuous – tried to comfort her by touching her hand.

At M——, a small village with a few houses and a general store, we disembarked. The station was a single room, with a partitioned area at the end holding a scale, telegraph gear, and a solitary chair.

The young station agent, with a shrewd expression, halted his work to inquire where we wanted to go.

"We're not going," McKnight quipped, "we're coming. Care for a cigar?"

Accepting the cigar, the agent eyed us.

"We have some questions," McKnight began, perching on the railing and pulling the chair forward for me. "Or, rather, this gentleman does."

"Hold on a moment," the agent interjected, peering out the window. "There's a hen in that crate choking itself."

He returned promptly and settled near a sawdust-filled box. "Proceed," he urged.

"To start," I began, "do you recall the day the Washington Flier derailed down here?"

"Do I!" he exclaimed. "Did Jonah recall the whale?"

"Were you on this platform when the first section went by?"

"I was."

"Did you see a man hanging to the last car's platform?"

"There was no one hanging there when it went past," he stated firmly. "I watched until it was out of sight."

"Did you notice a man, my size, carrying a small bag, wearing dark clothes and a derby hat?" I asked eagerly.

McKnight attempted to appear nonchalant, but I was genuinely anxious. It was clear the man had jumped somewhere in the mile of track just beyond.

"Well, yes," the agent cleared his throat. "When the crash happened, the operator at the next station sent messages along the wire, both ways. I received it here, and I was nearly losing my mind, although I knew it wasn't my fault.

"I was standing on the track, peering down since I couldn't leave the office, when this young bloke with light hair hobbles up and points at the smoke over there. 'What's that smoke from?' he asks. ''That's what remains of the Washington Flier,' I tell him, 'and I figure souls are rising in that smoke.'"

"'You mean the first section?' he said, turning a bit pale.

"'That's what I mean,' I said, 'shattered like kindling wood because Rafferty, on the second section, was in no mood to be late.'

"He extended his hand forward, and his bag fell with a bang.

"'Oh my God!' he exclaimed, collapsing onto the track.

"I got him inside the station, and he came to, but he kept moaning terribly. He'd sprained his ankle. Once he was a bit better, I got him a ride in Carter's milk wagon to the Carter place, where he stayed for a while."

"Is that the whole story?" I inquired.

"That's it… or, no, there's something else. Around noon that day, one of the Carter twins showed up with a note from him, asking me to send a long-distance message to someone in Washington."

"To whom?" I asked eagerly.

"I can't quite recall the name, but the message was that this guy – Sullivan was his name – was at M———, and if the person had escaped the wreck, would he come see him."

"He wouldn't have sent that to me," I told McKnight, a bit disheartened. "His intention would be to steer clear of me."

"There could be reasons," McKnight assessed thoughtfully. "Perhaps he hadn't found the documents then."

"Was the name Blakeley?" I probed.

"It might have been, I can't say for sure. But the man wasn't there, and there was lots of commotion. I couldn't hear well. After about thirty minutes, the other twin appeared, saying the gentleman was in quite a state and didn't want the message delivered."

"He's gone, I assume?"

"Yes. He limped down here in about three days and took the noon train back to the city."

It was almost certain now that our man, having injured himself somewhat during his leap, had stayed at the farmhouse until he was fit to travel. To be sure, we decided to visit the Carter place.

I handed the station agent a five-dollar bill, which he rolled up with a few others and stashed away. As we turned a bend in the road, I looked back, and he was watching us with curiosity.

It wasn't until we ascended the hill and turned onto the path leading to the Carter place that I realized where we were headed. Despite the different approach, I recognized the farmhouse instantly. It was the very one where Alison West and I had breakfasted nine days earlier. Due to the new strain between us, I refrained from mentioning this to McKnight. I wondered later if he had any inkling. I noticed him closely examining the gate-post, which had featured in one of our mysteries, but he didn't ask a thing. After that, he grew unusually reserved, letting me handle most of the conversation.

We opened the front gate of the Carter place and ambled up the walkway. Two scruffy kids, nearly identical down to their freckles and squints, were playing in the yard.

"Is your mom around?" I inquired.

"Front room. Just walk in," they echoed in unison.

Approaching the porch, we heard voices and halted. Though I knocked, those within, engrossed in a spirited, mostly one-sided discussion, offered no reply.

"'In the front room. Just walk in,'" McKnight mimicked, then entered.

Inside the stifling farm parlor, two figures were sitting. One, a pleasant woman in a checkered apron, stood, a bit flustered, to greet us. She didn't recognize me, for which I was thankful. Yet, our focus was on a little man seated at a table, writing diligently. It was Hotchkiss!

As soon as he saw us, he rose with visible unease. "Fascinating case, you know," he stammered, "I took the liberty…"

"Wait a second," McKnight cut in abruptly, "did you make any inquiries at the station?"

"I made some," he confessed. "Last night, I attended the theater – a bit of relaxation, you see – and the sight of a movie picture there, triggered a new line of thinking. Probably the same lead brought you gentlemen here. The station agent provided me with quite a bit of information."

"That rascal," McKnight exclaimed. "And I bet you paid him too, right?"

"I gave him five dollars," he admitted, sounding apologetic. Mrs. Carter, sensing trouble in the yard, left, and Hotchkiss folded up his papers.

"I believe the man's identity is established," he declared. "Mr. Blakeley, what's your hat size?"

"Seven and a quarter," I replied.

"More evidence piling up," he said cheerfully. "On the night of the murder, you wore light gray silk undergarments with the second shirt button missing. Your hat bore 'L. B.' in gilt letters inside, and there was a tiny hole in one black sock."

"Hold on," McKnight protested. "If word gets to Mrs. Klopton that Mr. Blakeley was wrecked, robbed, or whatever happened, with a button missing and a hole in a sock, she'll threaten to retire to the Old Ladies' Home. I've heard her say that."

Mr. Hotchkiss, humorless as ever, regarded McKnight solemnly and proceeded. "I've examined the room where the man stayed, and it yielded nothing. However, I may have found a potential lead in the rubbish pile.

"Mrs. Carter mentioned that while unpacking his bag, she discovered torn fragments of a telegram inside the jacket of some pajamas. My deduction is that the pajamas belonged to him. Likely, he had them on when he made the switch."

I nodded in agreement. All I had retained of my own clothing was the pajamas I wore and my bathrobe.

"So, the telegram was his, not yours. I've got some pieces here, although some are missing. Still, I'm not discouraged."

He spread out a few bits of yellow paper, and we leaned in, intrigued. It looked something like this:

Man   with   p—   Get—   Br—

We spelled it out slowly.

"My interpretation," Hotchkiss proclaimed, "goes somewhat like this: The 'p.—' signifies one of two things: pistol – you recall the small pearl-handled one belonging to the victim – or it's pocketbook. I'm leaning toward the latter, as the pocketbook had been disturbed, while the pistol had not."

I grabbed the pieces of paper from the table and scribbled four words on it.

"Now," I said, rearranging them, "Mr. Hotchkiss, it so happens that I found one of these pieces of telegram on the train. I believed it was dropped by someone else, you see, but that's beside the point. If we arrange it this way, it almost makes sense. Complete the 'p.—' with the remaining letters, as I imagine it, and you have 'papers.' Then, add this fragment, and you get:

"'Man with papers (in) lower ten, car seven. Get (them).'"

McKnight clapped Hotchkiss on the back. "You're brilliant," he exclaimed. "Br- stands for Bronson, obviously. It's almost too straightforward. You see, Mr. Blakeley here had reserved lower ten, but discovered it was occupied by the man who was later murdered there. The perpetrator was evidently an associate of Bronson's, and in trying to get the papers we have the motive for the crime."

"However, some matters still need explanation," Mr. Hotchkiss noted, wiping his glasses and slipping them on. "For instance, Mr. Blakeley, that piece of chain has me perplexed."

I avoided looking at McKnight. My hand, collecting the torn paper fragments, was trembling. It appeared that this astute little man was about to involve the girl, despite my intentions.

Chapter Eighteen
A NEW WORLD

Hotchkiss jotted down the bits of telegram and stood.

"Well," he said, "we've made progress. We've located where the murderer left the train, pinpointed what day he went to Baltimore, and, most importantly, unearthed a motive for the crime."

"Talk about irony of fate," remarked McKnight as he stood up, "a man kills for certain papers he thinks someone is carrying, finds that someone hasn't got them after all, changes berths to divert suspicion, and by sheer luck, ends up with the very papers he was after, swapping bags and all. Quite fortunate for him."

"Still," Hotchkiss interjected skeptically, "why did he faint upon hearing about the wreck? And what about that frantic telephone message the station agent sent for him, and was afterwards just as franticly countermanded?"

"We'll grill him about that when we catch him," declared McKnight. We had moved to the porch, and Hotchkiss had stowed his notebook. The mother of the twins followed us to the steps.

"Oh my goodness," she exclaimed energetically, "I nearly forgot to mention! I had the young man lie down with a spice poultice on his ankle; my mom was all for spice poultices. Works wonders for croup! Then I took the kids to see the wreck. It was Sunday, and my husband was at church – he's been devout since he took the pledge nine years ago. On the way, I encountered a man and a woman who looked like death warmed over. Sent them right here for breakfast and a chance to freshen up. Always believed soap does more good than spirits after a shock."

Hotchkiss listened absentmindedly; McKnight was humming softly, gazing at the field, a gap in the woods revealing telegraph poles and the railroad.

"Must've been around noon when we returned," she continued, "wanted the kids to witness it all, since it's unlikely they'll see another wreck like that. Rows of…"

"Approximately noon?" I interrupted, "And then?"

"The young man upstairs was awake," she went on, "hammering away at his door like a man possessed. And get this, it was locked from the outside!" she paused dramatically.

"I'd be keen to examine that lock," Hotchkiss promptly chimed in, but for some reason, the woman hesitated.

"I'll bring down the key," she offered, and vanished. When she reappeared, she presented a basic, inexpensive door key.

"We had to break the lock," she said, "and the key didn't turn up for two days. Then one of the twins found the turkey gobbler trying to swallow it… It's been cleaned since," she reassured Hotchkiss, who seemed ready to drop it.

"You think he locked the door himself and tossed the key out the window?" the little man queried.

"The windows have mosquito netting, nailed on. My husband blamed the kids, and maybe it was Obadiah. He's the quiet type, and you can't predict his moves."

"He's about to choke, isn't he?" McKnight commented casually, "Is that Obadiah?"

Mrs. Carter scooped up the boy and playfully turned him upside down while chatting. "He's always at it," she remarked, giving him a shake. "Whenever something's missing, we check if Obadiah's turning black in the face." She gave another shake, and the quarter I'd given him shot out like a bullet. Then we got ready to head back to the station.

From my vantage point, I could peer into the cheerful farmhouse kitchen where Alison West and I had enjoyed our outdoor breakfast. I glanced at the table with mixed feelings, and then, slowly, the significance of something on it dawned on me. Still in its packaging, apparently just opened, was a hat box, and extending over the box's edge was a vibrant green ribbon.

Using the excuse of needing to ask Mrs. Carter a few more questions, I let the others go ahead. I observed them as they strolled down the flagstone walkway; saw McKnight pause to inspect the gateposts and noted the quick glance he cast back at the house. Then I turned to Mrs. Carter.

"I'd like to speak with the young lady upstairs," I requested.

She threw her hands up in a swift gesture of surrender. "I've done all I can," she exclaimed. "She might not be too thrilled, but… she's in the room above the parlor."

Eagerly, I ascended the ladder-like stairs, arriving in the hallway covered in a ragged carpet. Two doors stood open, revealing interiors of four-poster beds and tall dressers. The door to the room above the parlor was nearly closed. I hesitated in the hallway – did I have the right to intrude on her? Yet she resolved my quandary by flinging open the door and confronting me.

"I… I apologize, Miss West," I stumbled, "I suddenly realize I've been incredibly impolite. I noticed the hat downstairs and I… I guessed—"

"The hat!" she exclaimed. "I should've expected that. Does Richey know I'm here?"

"I don't believe so." I began to descend the stairs again, then paused. "The truth is," I explained, attempting to justify myself, "I'm in a rather messy situation lately, and I might do rash things. It's not out of the question that I'll be arrested, in a day or so, for the murder of Simon Harrington."

"Murder!" she echoed. "So they've finally found you!"

"I don't see it as more than a minor inconvenience," I fibbed. "They won't be able to convict me, you see. Most of the witnesses are deceased."

She wasn't fooled for an instant. She approached me and leaned against the stair rail, both hands grasping it. "I understand the gravity of the situation," she said calmly. "My grandfather will leave no stone unturned, and he can be ruthless, ruthless indeed. But," she locked eyes with me as I stood below her on the stairs, "there might come a time – soon – when I'll be able to help you. I'll probably be reluctant; I'm quite the coward, Mr. Blakeley. However, I will try." she managed a faint smile.

"I'd appreciate your letting *me* assist *you*," I said unsteadily. "Let's strike a deal: we help each other!"

The girl shook her head, a sad smile on her lips. "I'm only as unhappy as I deserve to be," she confessed.

When I protested and moved closer, she stepped back, hands outstretched before her. "Why don't you ask me all the questions you have?" she demanded, her voice wavering. "Oh, I already know them. Or are you too scared to ask?"

I looked at her, the lines around her eyes, the tiredness around her mouth. Then I extended my hand. "Afraid!" I exclaimed as she placed her hand in mine. "There's nothing on this earth that I'm afraid of, except causing trouble for you. To question you would imply a lack of trust. I won't ask you anything. Perhaps someday, you might approach me and let me assist you."

The next instant, I was outside, embraced by the radiant sunshine. Birds sang songs of joy, and I walked unsteadily through clouds painted in rainbow hues. I passed by the twins, now resembling cherubs, swinging on the gate. It was a new world I entered that morning, leaving the Carter farmhouse, for… I had kissed her!

Chapter Nineteen
AT THE NEXT TABLE

AMERICAN PLAN – In the early 1900s, when this novel is set, hotels regularly offered meals with their accommodations. This service was known as the "American Plan," and provided three meals a day to each guest. Some establishments would, instead, offer only breakfast, commonly known as the "European Plan."

McKnight and Hotchkiss strolled leisurely down the road as I caught up with them. As usual, the little man was engrossed in some intricate mental puzzle.

"Here's the thought," he explained, his brow furrowed in concentration, "if a left-handed guy, positioned like the man in the movie picture, jumps from a car, is it likely he'd sprain his right ankle? When a right-handed person readies for a jump like that, my theory is they'd hold on with their right hand and land on their right foot at the right moment. Of course…"

"I'd assume," McKnight interjected, "though I'm no expert, that someone either ambidextrous or with one arm would be more prone to land on their head leaping from the Washington Flier."

"Anyway," I added, "what's the significance of whether Sullivan used his left or right hand? One pair of handcuffs would incapacitate both hands."

Typical of him when his cherished theories were challenged, Hotchkiss appeared affronted.

"My dear sir," he protested, "don't you grasp the relevance to the case? How was the murder victim lying when he was discovered?"

"On his back," I responded promptly, "head pointing toward the engine."

"Exactly," he countered, "and then what? Your heart lies beneath your fifth intercostal space, and for a right-handed strike to reach it, the blow would've gone either down or straight in.

"But, gentlemen, the dagger entered from below the heart, thrusting upwards! As Harrington lay with his head toward the engine, a person in the aisle must have used their left hand."

McKnight's gaze met mine, and he winked discreetly as I subtly switched the hat I was carrying to my right hand. Despite considerable conditioning, hereditary traits still play a role for me; I throw with my left hand, play tennis with my left hand, and even carve with my left hand. However, Hotchkiss was too engrossed in his theories to notice my actions.

We made it just in time for our train back to Baltimore, but McKnight took advantage of a second's delay to go warmly shake hands with the station agent. "I must commend you," he beamed. "Talent like yours is wasted here. You should've been a city police officer, my friend."

The agent seemed somewhat uncertain. "The young lady was the one who told me to keep quiet," he said.

McKnight glanced at me, gave the agent's hand a final shake, and boarded the train. Yet, I knew without a doubt that he had guessed the reason behind my delay.

The ride back home was notably quiet. Hotchkiss was absorbed in his notes, occasionally making additions, while Richey and I exchanged few words. Just before disembarking the train, Richey turned to me. "I guess she was the one who tied the key to the gate?"

"Likely. I didn't ask her," I responded.

"Strange, her locking that guy in," he mused.

"I'm sure there was a valid reason for it all. And Richey, you really shouldn't be so suspicious," I said, defending her.

"But just yesterday you were the one full of suspicion," he countered, and our conversation lapsed into silence.

By the time we reached Washington, it was late. Mrs. Klopton had a penchant for punctuality at meals, a tyranny I respected along with several others. There were certain concessions that deserved to be made in return for faithful service. Thus, given that my dinner hour of seven had long passed, McKnight and I opted for a local restaurant that prepared chicken a la King quite admirably. Hotchkiss, always frugal, headed to a small hotel where he was staying on the American plan.

"No, thank you. I want to mull over a few things," he explained when I invited him to join us, "plus, it makes no sense to dine out when I pay the same, dinner or no dinner, at my current lodging."

The day had been sweltering, and despite the attempts of palms and fans to evoke a sense of countryside verdure and breezes, the first-floor dining room was stifling. Additionally, it was crowded with the usual summertime patrons. After enduring a few moments in a particularly warm corner, we moved to a cooler upstairs dining area, where we comfortably settled by a window.

In a corner nearby, a group of boys on their way back to school were playfully teasing a sweaty waiter, a spectacle that suited so much McKnight's taste, that he insisted on going over to join them. But their table was full, and that kind of amusement had lost its appeal for me.

Not far from us, a rather plump middle-aged man, flushed from the heat, was boisterously amusing a disinterested young woman across from him. A lone female journalist dined at the adjacent table, the latest edition of the newspaper propped up by her water bottle, her hat positioned on the table's edge for relief from the heat. The scene reminded me of an eclectic gathering of Bohemian individuals.

I casually scanned the room while McKnight ordered our meal. Suddenly, my attention was drawn to the table next to ours. Two individuals sat there, so engrossed in conversation that they failed to notice our presence. The woman's face was concealed beneath her hat as she absentmindedly traced the pattern on the tablecloth with her fork. However, the man's features were clearly illuminated by the lit candles on the table. It was Bronson!

"Looks like he's under some pressure, doesn't he?" McKnight remarked, holding up the wine list as if consulting it. "And who's the woman?"

"Got me," I replied, adopting the same casual tone.

When our chicken dish arrived, I found my attention occasionally drawn to the preoccupied couple nearby. Clearly, their conversation had taken an unpleasant turn. Bronson was hardly eating, and the woman seemed to have lost her appetite entirely. Eventually, he abruptly stood up, pushed his chair back noisily, handed money to the waiter, and left the scene in a huff.

The woman sat motionless for a moment. Then, seemingly resolved to make the best of it, she began slowly eating her meal. However, the quarrel had clearly dampened her appetite. Soon she pushed her chair back and surveyed the room.

In that moment, I caught my first real glimpse of her face, and I must admit it startled me. It was the same elegant woman from the Ontario, the same woman who had been cowering on the roadside, holding pebbles and with a bleeding cut over her eye. I could discern the scar now, a small mark about an inch long, a reddish glint amidst layers of makeup.

Unexpectedly, she turned and directed her gaze straight at me. After a brief moment of uncertainty, she nodded her head, fixing her eyes on mine with a coolly insolent stare. She glanced at McKnight briefly, then returned her attention to me. When her gaze shifted away again, I felt a sense of relief.

"Who's that?" McKnight whispered, leaning in.

"Ontario," I mouthed more than uttered the word. His eyebrows shot up, and his curiosity shifted to the figure in the black gown.

My appetite waned considerably. The situation was growing increasingly precarious for me. I realized that this woman could, if she chose to and had a motive, potentially have me arrested on a serious charge. With just a word from her to the police, polite surveillance could quickly escalate into active interference.

Furthermore, she could testify to seeing me shortly after the train wreck, accompanied by a young woman from the murdered man's car. This might potentially involve Alison West in the case as well.

No wonder I lost my appetite. The woman across from me showed no haste to leave, lingering over a demitasse, and then sitting with her elbow on the table and her chin in her hand. She observed the room with an air of solemnity, her dark eyes shifting over the changing groups.

The noise from the table with the college boys grew a bit louder, the flushed man turned a purplish hue as he lumbered off behind his slender companion, and the lone newspaper woman donned her practical hat and departed. Still, the woman at the adjacent table remained seated.

It was a welcome relief when the meal was over. We put on our hats, preparing to leave the room, when a waiter approached and tapped me on the arm. "I apologize, sir," he said, "but the lady at the table near the window, the one dressed in black, sir, would like to have a word with you."

I glanced down the rows of tables to where the woman sat by herself, chin resting on her hand, her penetrating black eyes once again fixed insolently on me.

"I'll have to go," I hastily informed McKnight. "She knows all about that affair, and she could be a formidable adversary."

"I don't like her gaze," McKnight commented, giving her a quick glance. "Perhaps you should charm her a bit. Good luck."

Chapter Twenty
THE NOTES AND A DEAL

I approached the woman's table slowly. She greeted me with an odd smile and gestured to the vacant chair, where Bronson had been sitting.

"Take a seat, Mr. Blakeley," she said. "I'd like to have a few words with you."

"Sure." I sat across from her and glanced at the cuckoo clock on the wall. "I am sorry, but I have only a few minutes, though."

She chuckled slightly and opened a sparkly black fan. "Here's the thing," she began, fanning herself. "I believe we're on the verge of striking a deal."

"A deal?" I raised an eyebrow. "You seem to know my name. I don't have that advantage."

"I'm Mrs. Conway," she introduced herself, brushing a crumb off the table with an over-manicured finger.

The name wasn't a surprise. I had guessed she might be the woman Bronson was having an affair with, according to rumors. The same rumors tied her also to less pleasant matters.

"Our last encounter was in less than fortunate circumstances," she continued. "I've been struggling since that awful day. And you… you had a broken arm, I believe."

"Yeah, still dealing with that," I joked weakly. "But surviving was a bit of luck. We can be thankful for that much."

"I suppose," she mused, glancing toward the exit where her companion had left.

"You sent for me," I said.

"Indeed." She straightened up. "Now, Mr. Blakeley, have you found those papers?"

"Papers? What papers?" I stalled, needing time to think.

"Let's drop the pretense, Mr. Blakeley," she said calmly. "First, a reminder. The Pittsburgh police are seeking the survivors of the Ontario train wreck. There are three of us: you, the young woman you left with, and me. That wreck was fortunate for you, I'd say."

I nodded, wordlessly.

"You were in a tight spot at the time of the collision," she continued, eyeing me with a smug smile. "Accused of a heinous crime, if I recall. Strong evidence against you, right? I remember a dagger, the victim's wallet, and some other rather unsavory items in your possession."

I was caught off guard for a moment. "You also remember," I interjected swiftly, "that a man vanished from the train, taking my belongings, clothes, and documents."

"I recall you making that *claim*," she retorted, her tone dripping with skepticism.

I regretted my hasty words; this wasn't the time for a defense. "But there's one factor you've overlooked," I said coolly. "The man who left the train will be found."

"You've found him?" Her posture leaned forward, "I knew it. I said as much."

I regretted, again, my impulsive words. "We're going to find him," I asserted, with more confidence than I felt. "We can present evidence anytime that a man disembarked from the Flier a few miles from the wreck. I'm certain we'll locate him."

"But you haven't found him yet?" Her disappointment was clear. "Very well. Now, let's talk about our deal. I'm not naive," she declared, her tone mocking.

"I never claimed you were," I responded, and she smirked.

"How flattering you are!" she said. "Now for the premises. You head to Pittsburgh with four notes from Mechanics' National Bank to have Mr. Gilmore, who's unwell, declare his endorsement of them forged. On your way back, two things happen to you: you lose your stuff, including the notes, and you get accused of murder. The circumstances were most unusual, and the evidence… pretty strong."

I was totally at her mercy, but I tried to keep calm.

"Now, let's talk deal…" she leaned in and whispered, "A fair deal, you know. Once you hand over those four notes to me, the hit to my head erases all memory of that dreadful morning. I'm the sole witness, and I'll stay quiet. Got it? They'll call off their dogs."

The idea seemed surreal, my mind was buzzing. "But," I countered, stalling for time, "I don't have the notes. I can't give you what I don't possess."

"You've managed to have the case continued," she snapped. "You're counting on finding them. And another thing," she added slowly, studying my expression, "if you don't find them soon, Bronson will. He's been offered them already, but at a steep price."

"But," I stammered, confused, "why approach me? If Bronson will acquire them anyway…"

She snapped her fan shut, her expression turning unpleasant. "You're quite dense," she said rudely. "*I* want those papers, not for Andy Bronson, but for myself."

"So, your idea is that you think you've got me cornered, and if I locate those papers and hand them to you, you'll release me. Essentially, our dear friend Bronson would be in a similar predicament," I summarized.

She affirmed with a nod.

"However," I continued, studying her intently, "the papers would only be useful to you for a limited time. If they're not handed over to the state's attorney reasonably soon, the case would have to be dropped due to lack of evidence."

"A week should suffice, I suppose," she replied slowly. "Are you on board with this?"

I laughed, though my mood wasn't particularly cheerful. "No, I won't agree to that. I fully intend to come across those papers soon, and when I do, I'll promptly deliver them to the state's attorney."

She abruptly stood up, scraping her chair loudly and drawing curious glances from around the room. "You're even more of a fool than I thought," she jeered, and stormed away from the table.

Chapter Twenty-One
McKNIGHT'S THEORY

I confess I was taken aback. The people at nearby tables briefly glanced my way before diverting their attention.

I got my hat and left in a rather uncomfortable state of mind. I had little doubt that she would promptly inform the police about her knowledge, unless she decided to allow a day or two for me to reconsider.

As I waited for a streetcar, I reviewed the situation. Two streetcars passed by in the opposite direction, and on the first one, I spotted Bronson with his hat low and a somber demeanor. Was it just my imagination, or was the small man huddled in the corner of the back seat Hotchkiss? A smile crept onto my face as the car rolled away. The vigilant little man resembled a terrier, always on the scent and searching in every direction.

I found McKnight at the Incubator, sleeves rolled up, diligently using a manicure file on his car horn. "This horn is the absolute worst," he grumbled without looking up as I entered. "It's absolutely refusing to make a sound." He struck the horn with frustration, finally coaxing out a feeble, raspy croak.

"Sounds like it has a bad case of croup," I quipped. "My sister-in-law swears by camphor and goose grease for that, or maybe a spice poultice?"

But McKnight only appreciates his own brand of humor. He flung the horn into a corner with a clatter and plopped into a chair with a sulky air.

"Now," I began, "if you've finished your horn manicure session, I'll tell you about my conversation with the lady in black."

"What's the trouble?" McKnight asked lazily. "Are the police shadowing her too?"

"Not exactly. Actually, Rich, things have taken a turn for the worse."

Stogie entered, bringing a few creature comforts. Once he left, I recounted the events.

"You must remember," I said, "that I had seen this woman before the morning of the crash. She was at the Pullman ticket counter when I was. Then, when the murder came to light the next day, she became hysterical, and I gave her some whisky. The third time I saw her, until tonight, was when she was crouched by the roadside after the wreck."

McKnight slid back in his chair until he rested on the small of his back and propped his feet onto the large reading table.

"This is quite the conundrum," he mused. "It's almost too good of a situation for an ordinary lawyer. It practically begs for a dramatic treatment. Naturally, you can't accept; and by refusing, you risk jail time and dragging Alison into the spotlight, which is out of the question. You mentioned she was at the Pullman counter when you were?"

"Yes, I bought her ticket. Gave her lower berth eleven."

"And you took berth ten?"

"Lower ten."

McKnight straightened up, looking at me intently. "So she thought you were in berth ten."

"I suppose so, if she even considered it."

"Think about it, though." McKnight's excitement was palpable. "What's the implication here? Mrs. Conway knows you took the notes to Pittsburgh. Chances are, she follows you there, hoping for a chance to acquire them, either for Bronson or herself.

"Absolutely nothing happened during the journey to or the day in Pittsburgh. However, she learns your berth number when you purchase it at the Pullman counter there, and she sees her opportunity. No one could have predicted that the inebriated man would crawl into your berth.

"This is my take: She urgently wanted those notes, still does, not for Bronson's sake, but as leverage over him for some reason. In the dead of night, when everything is quiet, she slips behind the curtains of berth ten, where the man's snores indicate his slumber. You mentioned he snored?"

"He did," I confirmed. "But…"

"Now hold on and hear me out. In the darkness, she fumbles around cautiously, eventually locating the wallet under the pillow. Can't you visualize it?" He was leaning forward, brimming with excitement, and I could almost visualize the macabre scene he was portraying.

"She extracts the wallet. Then, perhaps recalling the alligator bag, she reaches out in the hope that the notes might be there, instead of the wallet. Suddenly, the man stirs and seizes the nearest object, possibly her necklace, which snaps. She drops the wallet and tries to flee, but his grip tightens around her right hand.

"This all happens in silence; the man remains in a stupor. Yet, he holds her firmly. Then comes the tragedy. She has to escape, with the realization that the car will soon be roused. A woman on such an errand wouldn't be without some form of weapon, in this case, a dagger, which, unlike a gun, makes no noise.

"With a swift thrust – she's a strong and bold woman – she strikes. Maybe Hotchkiss is correct about the blow coming from her left hand. Harrington could have restrained her right hand, or she might have held the dagger in her left hand while groping with her right. As the man topples back and his grasp slackens, she stands and attempts to flee. The swaying of the car almost propels her into your berth, and, trembling with fear, she cowers behind the curtains of berth ten until all falls quiet. Then, noiselessly, she returns to her own berth."

I nodded, absorbed in his explanation.

"It fits partly, at least," I admitted. "In the morning, when she realized the crime had not only been futile but she had also searched the wrong berth and killed the wrong person – when she saw me emerging unharmed just as she was bracing herself for the sight of my lifeless body – she succumbed to hysteria. As I said, I gave her some whisky.

"It does seem like a plausible theory. But, like the Sullivan scenario, there are a couple of discrepancies in the narrative. First, how do we account for the rest of that necklace chain ending up in Alison West's possession?" I asked.

"She might have picked it up from the floor."

"Let's assume that's possible," I said. "And I genuinely hope that's the case. But then, how do we explain the victim's wallet being inside the sealskin bag? And the dagger? And what about the bloodstains?"

"What's the point," McKnight asked with a hint of frustration, "of me constructing these elegant theories only for you to tear them down? Let's take it to Hotchkiss. Maybe he can deduce the murderer's fingernail shape from the bloodstains."

"Hotchkiss isn't a fool," I replied reassuringly. "Beneath all his theories lies a solid core of common sense. And we can't forget, Rich, that neither of our theories accounts for the woman at Dr. Van Kirk's hospital. Your vivid portrayal doesn't explain Alison West's involvement in the case or the torn telegram scraps found in Sullivan's pajama pocket. It's like assembling a clock and having half the gears left over."

"Enough, just go home," McKnight retorted in exasperation. "I'm no Edgar Allan Poe. Why bother asking me things if you're going to be so particular?"

In one of his swift shifts of mood, he reached for his guitar. "Listen to this," he declared. "It's a Hawaiian song about a portly lady, and how she fell off her mule."

Despite the lighthearted lyrics, his voice as I descended the stairs held a somber note. I paused on the lower level, listening. His singing halted as abruptly as it had begun.

Chapter Twenty-Two
AT THE BOARDING-HOUSE

- NOTES -

SHOVEL VS. SPADE – Yes! There is a difference! While most people – even in 1910 – used the terms interchangeably, shovels are primarily used for moving material like dirt and snow whereas spades are primarily used for digging holes and trenches with straight sides.

A PRIMROSE BY THE RIVER'S BRIM, A YELLOW PRIMROSE WAS TO HIM, AND NOTHING MORE! –This verse comes from the poem "Peter Bell, A Tale in Verse," a long narrative poem by William Wordsworth, published in 1819.

I hadn't been home for thirty-six hours, not since the morning of the previous day. Johnson was nowhere to be seen, so I let myself in quietly with my latchkey. It was almost midnight, and I had barely settled in the library when the doorbell rang. To my surprise, Hotchkiss, somewhat out of breath, appeared at the door.

"Come in, Mr. Hotchkiss," I invited. "I thought you were headed home to get some rest."

"So I was, so I was," he took a seat by my reading lamp and wiped his brow. "And yet, it's nearly midnight, and I'm more awake than ever. I've seen Sullivan, Mr. Blakeley."

"You have!"

"I certainly have," he declared solemnly.

"You were trailing Bronson around eight o'clock. Was that when it happened?"

"Something along those lines. As I was leaving you at the restaurant entrance, I almost bumped into a plainclothes detective from the central office. We're acquainted; he's taken me along on a couple of intriguing cases, and he's familiar with my interest. And you probably know him too. It was Arnold, the detective the district attorney had watching Bronson."

Given that Johnson was occupied elsewhere, I had personally requested Arnold's assistance. I nodded.

"Arnold stopped me right away. He mentioned he'd been tracking Bronson since early morning and hadn't had a chance to eat lunch. Bronson seems to have lost his appetite these days. I made note of that immediately, as it indicated he was troubled by the man with the notes."

"It might imply other things," I proposed. "Perhaps indigestion."

Hotchkiss brushed off my suggestion. "Anyway, Arnold had a hunch that Bronson might attempt to give him the slip that evening, so he asked me to hang around the private entrance while he grabbed a quick meal across the street. Considering Bronson arrived with a lady, we assumed they'd leisurely dine, giving Arnold ample time to return."

"What about your own dinner?" I inquired with curiosity.

"Sir," he declared pompously, "if you think the matter of dinner would even cross Wilson Budd Hotchkiss' mind at a time like this, you've gravely misjudged me."

He was a frail little man, and tonight, he appeared pale from the heat and exertion.

"Did you manage to have lunch?" I asked.

He seemed a bit embarrassed by that question. "I… I must admit, Mr. Blakeley, the day's events had so captivated my attention…"

"Well," I interjected, "I won't stand by while you collapse from exhaustion. Just give me a moment."

Returning to the pantry, I was met with locked doors and empty dishes. However, in the basement kitchen, I located two unappetizing cold chops, dry bread, and a piece of cake, wrapped in a napkin. Given its appearance, it seemed intended for the stable coachman out back. There were no trays to be found; everything except the chairs and tables appeared locked away, and not a napkin, knife, or fork in sight.

Although the meal was unappealing, Hotchkiss devoured his cold chops and gnawed on the crusts as though ravenous, all the while sharing his story.

"I had only been there a short while," he recounted, holding a chop in one hand and the cake in the other, "when Bronson rushed out and crossed the street. He's a tall man, Mr. Blakeley, and it was a challenge keeping up with him. I breathed a sigh of relief when he hopped onto a passing streetcar. However, as I was trailing well behind, I had to sprint to catch him. He had left the lady behind.

"Once on the streetcar, we essentially rode back and forth along the entire route. I suppose he was merely passing time, as he occasionally glanced at his watch. When I managed to catch a glimpse of his face, it gave me a sense of… well, unease. He could have crushed me like a fly, sir."

I had given Mr. Hotchkiss a glass of wine, and his appearance had visibly improved. After taking a moment to savor it, he declined a refill with a dismissive gesture and continued his narrative.

"Around nine o'clock, or perhaps a bit later, he got off near Washington Circle. He proceeded down a residential street, turned left after a couple of blocks, and rang a doorbell. By the appearance of the place, I surmised it was a boarding house.

"I waited a few minutes, then rang the bell myself. A maid answered, and I inquired about Mr. Sullivan. Naturally, no such person resided there.

"I apologized, explaining I was looking for a new boarder. She was certain there was no such boarder in the house, but she did mention a recent arrival on the third floor. She believed his name was Stuart.

"'My friend has a cousin with that name,'" I explained. "'I'll just head up and see for myself.'

"Although she offered to accompany me, I said it wasn't necessary. She told me it was the bedroom and sitting-room on the third floor front, and I made my way up.

"I encountered a couple of men on the stairs, yet they paid me no mind. Boarding houses are rather easy to enter."

"They're not always so easy to leave," I added, which visibly annoyed him.

"Upon reaching the third floor," he continued, "I produced a set of keys and positioned myself near a door close to the ones the maid had indicated. I could hear voices coming from one of the front rooms, but could not understand what they said. There wasn't a heated argument, but a consistent murmur. Bronson then swung the door open. Had he ventured into the corridor, he would have spotted me fitting a key into the door before me. However, he spoke before coming out.

"'You're behaving like a lunatic,'" he said. "'You know I can secure those things one way or another; I won't resort to threats. It's unnecessary. You know me.'

"'It would be useless,'" the other man responded. "'I assure you, I haven't laid eyes on those notes for ten days.'

"'But you will,'" Bronson retorted angrily. "'You're standing in your own way, that's all. If you're stalling, hoping I'll raise my offer, you're mistaken. This is my final offer.'

"'I couldn't accept it even if it were for a million,'" the man inside the room stated. "'I suppose I would if I could. The best of us have our price.'

"Bronson then slammed the door and stormed past me down the corridor.

"After a couple of minutes, I knocked on the door, and a tall man about your build, Mr. Blakeley, opened it. He had a very fair complexion, with a clean-shaven face and blue eyes. You might call him a handsome man.

"'I apologize for intruding,'" I said. "'Could you kindly tell me which room belongs to Mr. Johnson? Mr. Francis Johnson?'

"'I can't say,'" he replied courteously. "'I've only been here a few days.'

"I thanked him and left, but I had had a good look at him. I believe I'd be able to identify him anywhere."

I took a moment to contemplate the situation. "But what did he mean by stating he hadn't seen the notes in ten days? And why is Bronson making these offers?"

"I suspect he was lying," Hotchkiss mused. "Bronson hasn't met his terms."

"It's a significant development, Mr. Hotchkiss, and I'm truly grateful for your efforts," I expressed. "Now, if you can locate any of my belongings in that man's room, we can have him charged with theft and at least bring him into our grasp. I'm heading to Cresson tomorrow to trace his movements a bit. However, I'll return in a couple of days, and we can begin gathering together these scattered threads."

Hotchkiss rubbed his hands together with delight. "That's the spirit," he declared. "That's precisely what we should do, Mr. Blakeley. We'll gather the threads ourselves; involving the police too soon may only entangle the matter further. I'm not naturally vindictive, but when a person like Sullivan not only commits a murder but goes to great lengths to shift the blame onto an innocent man... well, I say *hunt him down*, sir!"

"You're fully convinced, I presume, that Sullivan is the culprit?" I inquired.

"Who else?" He peered at me over his glasses, exuding an air of unassailable certainty.

"Very well, listen to this," I began, narrating in detail my encounter with Bronson at the restaurant, the proposition offered by Mrs. Conway, and finally, McKnight's fresh theory. While he seemed impressed, he remained far from entirely persuaded.

"Quite an imaginative narrative," he remarked dryly, "though it fits the available evidence only to a certain extent. It leaves gaps in the story. What about the stains in lower berth seven, the dagger, and the wallet? Haven't we even got motive in that telegram from Bronson?"

"True," I conceded, "but then there's that bit of chain…"

"Pshaw," he interrupted dismissively. "Perhaps Sullivan wore glasses with a chain, much like yourself. The absence of evidence doesn't necessarily negate its existence."

And there I made a mistake; partial revelations often lead to missteps. I couldn't disclose the broken chain inside Alison West's gold purse.

By the time Hotchkiss departed at one o'clock, we had outlined a clear plan: Hotchkiss would search Sullivan's quarters and, if possible, gather evidence to justify his detention for theft, while I would head to Cresson.

Oddly enough, the following morning, when I entered the train, Hotchkiss was already onboard. Armed with a fresh notepad and sharpened pencil, he pushed his newspaper aside to make room for me.

"I had a change of plans, you see," he explained, brimming with enthusiasm. "It's not a knock on your intelligence, Mr. Blakeley, but your perspective lacks the professional eye, the analytical mind. Legal minds tend to label a spade a spade, even when it might actually be a shovel."

"'A primrose by the river's brim, A yellow primrose was to him, And nothing more!'"

I quoted as the train pulled away from the station.

Chapter Twenty-Three
A NIGHT AT THE LAURELS

- NOTES -

RUBBER BLANKET (OR RUBBER APRON) – A rubber covering used in horse buggies to protect the occupants from rain or snow.

DOUBLE-DUMMY BRIDGE – In the early 1900s, this was a popular two-handed form of bridge. At the beginning of the game, two dummy hands were shown, so both players had complete knowledge of the other's cards. The right play was therefore a matter of straightforward analysis, with no guess work involved.

EUCHRE – Euchre or eucre is a trick-taking card game that emerged in the United States in the early 19th century. It normally involves four players, two on each team, but some variations allow for two to nine players. Being a relatively simple trick game, as opposed to double-dummy bridge, Hotchkiss' question about whether the two games are similar signals that he's not much of a card player.

I dozed through most of the trip to Cresson, much to the annoyance of the little detective. He eventually struck up a chat with a friendly old priest, who was carrying a roll of dance music and surreptitious bundles resembling boxes of candies, on his way home to his convent school. From their conversation, I gathered that strange incidents had occurred at the convent, leading to the theft of vague items referred to as "under muslins." I fell asleep again but woke to find Hotchkiss showing the old priest a diagram on an envelope.

Hotchkiss said, "Considering this bolted window, and that one inaccessible, and if, as you say, the… er… garments were in a tub here at X, then, as you have the key to the other door... Did you say the convent dog remained quiet? And pardon the question, do you ever sleepwalk?"

The priest looked puzzled.

"Here's a suggestion," Hotchkiss said, leaning forward. "Check things out before calling the police. Sleepwalking is a peculiar thing. We might be truer versions of ourselves asleep than awake. Think about it. You spend the day in piety, prayers, and such, yet your subconscious sneaks you out at night to steal under muslins! Call it subliminal theft. Better inspect the roof."

I drifted off again. When I woke, Hotchkiss sat alone, and the priest, from a corner, stared dazedly at him over his breviary.

It was raining when we arrived in Cresson, a wind-blown rain that made the newsstand agent retreat indoors. Hotchkiss seemed oblivious to the weather and our bedraggled state as he walked up the main street. Or I should say *my* bedraggled state, as he looked increasingly excited, with brighter eyes, redder face, and a crisp collar.

I felt increasingly depressed. Spying on a woman was despicable in my book. Plus, I dreaded uncovering what I might learn. For a time, however, this promised to be a negligible quantity. The small mountain town was deserted due to the rain. Windows and doors were tightly shut, and dim light seeped from behind a few drawn shades. When Hotchkiss' umbrella turned inside out, I stopped.

"I don't know where you're headed," I snapped, "but I'm finding cover in ten seconds. I'm not amphibious."

I sought refuge in the nearest shelter, the entrance of a livery stable, and shook myself off like a dog. Hotchkiss wiped his collar with his handkerchief, revealing it unblemished and crisp.

"This place will do fine," he said, raising his voice over the rain's noise. "Gotta start somewhere."

I settled onto a backless chair just inside the door, staring out at the darkening street. The whole situation felt unreal. Doubts about the necessity and worth of the journey crept in now that I was there. Wet and uncomfortable, I pondered the task ahead. Around me, an irregular circle of mountains radiated from Cresson as the center, possibly spanning ten miles. Within it, I was to locate the abode of a woman whose first name eluded me, and a man who had thus far existed only as an illusion.

Hotchkiss had ventured into the steamy stable's interior, his voice mixing with the occasional thud of horse hooves. "Something light will do," he was saying. "Perhaps a runabout." He returned, rubbing his hands, followed by a thin man in overalls. "This is Mr. Peck, from Peck and Peck," he began. "He says the place we're seeking is roughly seven miles from town. The weather clearing up, don't you think?"

"No, it's not," I retorted irritably. "And we don't need a runabout, Mr. Peck. What we need is a fully sealed diving suit. Is there a car available?"

"Only personal vehicles. I can provide a good buggy with a rubber blanket. Mike, is the doctor's horse here?"

I'm still uncertain whether the bony roan we took that night across the mountains belonged to the doctor or not. If it did, the doctor might be skilled in medicine, but he doesn't know anything about a horse. Moreover, I hope he didn't require the beast on that wretched evening.

While they readied the horse, Hotchkiss shared his findings with me. "Six Curtises in town and nearby," he said. "A common family name around here. One of them works as a telegraph operator at the station. The person we're seeking is – or was –a wealthy widow with a brother named Sullivan. Both presumed dead in the Flier incident."

"Her brother," I repeated dully.

"You see," Hotchkiss continued, "three individuals were on that train that night: Miss West, Mrs. Curtis, and Sullivan. The two women had the drawing-room, Sullivan had lower seven. Our goal is to uncover who these people were, where they came from, whether Bronson was acquainted with them, and how Miss West got involved with them. She may have married Sullivan, for one thing."

A sense of gloom enveloped me. The roan was led reluctantly into the rain, Hotchkiss and I concealed behind the rubber blanket. The liveryman stood at the doorway, offering instructions. "You can't miss it," he concluded. "The name's on the gate, 'The Laurels.' The staff's still there. And if you're settling the estate," he shouted, "remember us, Peck and Peck."

Hotchkiss wasn't skilled at driving. The roan splashed through puddles, staining us with mud, which only fueled my growing irritation.

"What's our plan when we arrive?" I inquired, finally taking the reins with my one functional hand. "Get there at midnight and tell the servants we're there to ask about the family? This trip seems ridiculous. I should've stayed home."

The roan stumbled, prompting us to help it up and partially unharness it. Now our matches were gone, and the small bicycle lamp on the buggy flickered uncertainly. Covered in mud, panting from exertion, even Hotchkiss displayed a surly attitude. The rain, which had momentarily eased, now resumed, with lightning flashes revealing our isolated situation.

Another mile deepened our despondency, our drenched clothes a testament to the water's infiltration. The roan had injured its shoulder and was now dragging us in spasmodic jerks.

Then, through the rain-streaked window of the rubber blanket, I glimpsed a light. It glowed for about thirty seconds, but Hotchkiss missed it and was inclined to doubt me. Yet, within a couple of minutes, the roan limped to the roadside and stopped, and I spotted a break in the trees and an arched gate.

The gate was small, too narrow for the buggy. I maneuvered the horse beneath the trees for shelter and we got out. Hotchkiss secured the horse, leaving it hunched against the driving rain, forlorn and dejected. Then we proceeded towards the house.

The walk was lengthy. The path twisted and turned, at times we lost it. Oddly there were no lights ahead, although it was only ten o'clock — not very late. Hotchkiss moved slightly ahead of me, occasionally bumping into trees but locating the path twice as fast as I would have. Once, groping around a tree in the darkness, my hand unexpectedly landed on his shoulder, sending a shiver down my spine.

"What do you want me to do?" he protested when I remonstrated. "Hold up a red lantern? Wait! Did you hear that? Listen."

We both stood still, peering into the obscurity. The sharp rain pattering on the leaves had ceased, replaced by the subtle sound of footsteps in damp earth coming from just ahead. My grip tightened on Hotchkiss' shoulder as we listened cautiously. The footsteps were close and unmistakable. The next lightning flash revealed nothing in motion. The house stood before us, huge and unwelcoming, looming over a terrace, with an adjacent Italian garden. Darkness returned. Someone's teeth were chattering, and I suspected Hotchkiss, but he denied it.

"Though I'm not very comfortable, I'll admit," he confessed. "A moment ago, there was something breathing right beside me."

"Rubbish!" I dismissed his notion, taking his elbow and guiding him toward what I discerned to be the path to the Italian garden's steps. "I just saw a deer up ahead during the last flash — that's what you heard. By Jove, I hear wheels."

Pausing to listen, Hotchkiss placed his hand on something nearby. "Here's your deer," he remarked. "Bronze."

As we approached the house, the feeling of being watched that we had experienced in the park gradually dissipated. Tripping over flower beds, stumbling into a sun-dial, and grappling our way irritably through hedges and thorny banks, we eventually reached the steps and climbed the terrace.

At that moment, Hotchkiss stumbled over one of the two stone urns that flanked the entrance, each housing tall boxwood trees. He made no effort to get up: He sat in a puddle on the terrace's brick floor, clutching his leg and softly uttering curses.

The intermittent illumination provided by lightning was gone, and the house's outline remained invisible. We had no matches, but I soon realized that the windows were shuttered and the house was sealed. Hotchkiss, still seated, examined his injury, gently pulling down his stocking.

"By my soul," he eventually remarked, "I can't tell if this moisture is blood or rain. I believe I've broken a bone."

"Blood is thicker than water," I suggested. "Is it sticky? Try moving your toes."

A pause ensued. Hotchkiss moved his toes. In the meantime, I had located a knocker and I was making a lot of noise. Yet, there was no response except for the wind that mockingly flung wet leaves in our faces. Hotchkiss claimed to have heard a window sash being lifted, but my renewed assault on the knocker failed to have any effect.

"There's only one course of action," I concluded. "I'll head back and attempt to bring the buggy up for you. Can you walk?"

Hotchkiss reclined in his puddle, expressing doubt about his ability to move. He urged me to leave him behind and return to town without him, stating that he had no family and that he had probably contracted pneumonia and was dead already. Rolling my eyes, I set off to retrieve the horse.

If possible, the situation was worse than before. There was no lightning, and it was only by sheer luck that I found the small gate again. With a deep sigh of relief, followed by an equally lengthy exhalation of dismay, I realized I had found the hitching strap – but nothing was attached to its end! In a lull in the wind, I sensed the faint, eager rhythm of hooves headed towards the stable. So, for the second time, I trudged up the path to the Laurels, contemplating what I would say along the way.

I stumbled upon the house from a different angle, locating a veranda devoid of furniture but dry and seemingly sheltered. It offered a better alternative to the terrace, so I felt my way along the wall in an attempt to reach Hotchkiss. That's when I discovered the open window – an unexpected encounter with the soft drapery of an inner curtain, instead of the closed window I had anticipated.

I eventually located Hotchkiss around a corner of the stone wall and informed him that the horse was gone. He appeared unsettled but not defeated, suggesting that the horse must have chewed through the halter, since his knot couldn't possibly come undone. His enthusiasm about the open window was less than I had expected.

"It seems suspiciously like a trap," he remarked. "I'm telling you, someone was in the park below when we were climbing up. Humans possess a sixth sense that scientists overlook – a sense of proximity. And throughout the time you were away, someone has been observing me."

"I couldn't see you," I countered. "I can't even see you now. And your "sense of proximity" didn't help you with that flower pot."

In the end, he reluctantly agreed to accompany me. His lameness was evident, and I assisted him to the open window. The little man was filled with moral courage; it was only his physical condition that faltered. As we moved cautiously, he insisted on going through the window first.

"If it's a trap," he whispered, "I have two arms to your one, and besides, as I mentioned earlier, you've got more to live for. As for me, the government would simply lose an indifferent employee."

When he realized I was going first, he seemed slightly offended, but I paid no attention to his objections. I swung my legs over the windowsill and dropped. Realizing there was no floor beneath me, I attempted to grab onto the window frame with my good hand, but I was too slow. I plummeted about ten feet and landed with a crash. Though thoroughly shaken, miraculously, both my bandaged arm and my legs had remained unharmed.

"For heaven's sake," Hotchkiss called from above, "have you broken your spine?"

"No," I replied as steadily as I could, "just driven it up into my skull. There's a staircase here. I'm coming up to open another window."

Despite the eerie nature of the situation, I eventually accomplished the task. I stumbled into a room teeming with more tables than I could have imagined, tables that seemed to ambush and assail me. Once I managed to open a window, Hotchkiss crawled through, and we were finally indoors.

Our immediate concern was finding some light. After an exhaustive search, we deduced that the house had been wired for electricity, though at the moment there was no power. By chance, I stumbled upon a small table with smoking supplies and found a handful of matches. The first match illuminated the vastness of the room we were in and revealed an almost four feet tall brass candlestick by an open fireplace, supporting a correspondingly colossal candle. Hotchkiss noticed that the candle had recently been lit. He held the match close and examined it over his glasses.

"Within the last ten minutes," he announced impressively, "this candle has been burning. Look at the wax! And the wick! Both are soft."

"Perhaps it's due to the damp weather," I suggested unconvincingly, inching closer to the circle of light. A gust of wind suddenly blew in, causing the flame to flicker and almost die out. There was something almost comical about our haste in shutting the window and tending to the struggling flame.

The room had a distinctly ghostly appearance, adding an eerie touch to the already uncanny situation. The furniture was draped in white covers for the winter, and even the paintings were covered. Positioned between two windows, a bust on a pedestal – similarly wrapped – with one arm extended from its shroud, resembled an uncannily lifelike ghost, if such a thing is possible.

In the light of the candle, we looked at each other and found ourselves rather absurd. Hotchkiss was in the process of removing his wet shoes and preparing to get comfortable, while I casually hung my muddy raincoat over the ghost in the corner. Dressed in this makeshift manner, he had a rakish but significantly more comfortable appearance.

"The people who built this house," Hotchkiss remarked, surveying the vast expanse of the room, "must have purchased an entire mountain and built all over it. What a room!"

The space seemed to serve as a living room, although Hotchkiss dryly observed that it felt more like a dead one. It was likely around fifty feet long and twenty-five feet wide, featuring an impressive height with a domed ceiling. A gallery encircled the entire room, about fifteen feet above the floor. The candle's glow couldn't penetrate beyond the faint contours of the gallery rail, yet I suspected that smaller paintings adorned the wall there.

Hotchkiss had discovered a fire prepared in the grand fireplace, and within minutes, we were warming up before a cheerful blaze. In the radius of its light and warmth, we began to feel comfortable once more. However, the brightness only accentuated the shadows in the ghostly corners. Our conversation maintained a hushed tone as I smoked Russian cigarettes I found in a table drawer.

Given the lack of alternatives, we had decided to spend the night there. I proposed a game of double-dummy bridge, though I didn't insist when my companion inquired if it was similar to euchre. Gradually, as the ecclesiastical candle's glow waned in the firelight, drowsiness overtook us. I dragged a divan into the cozy area and settled down to sleep. Hotchkiss, claiming that his leg pain kept him awake, remained sitting by the fire, eyes wide open as he smoked his pipe.

I had no idea of how much time had passed when something abruptly lunged onto my chest. Startled, I jolted awake and jumped to my feet, causing a large Angora cat to thud onto the floor. The fire still burned brightly, and a scent of singed leather permeated the room, originating from Hotchkiss' shoes. The little detective was sound asleep, his extinguished pipe in his hand. The cat sat back on its haunches and wailed.

The curtain at the door to the hallway billowed slowly into the room and then settled. The cat gazed toward it and opened its mouth for another cry. I nudged it with my foot, but it remained rooted. Hotchkiss stirred restlessly, and his pipe clattered to the floor.

The cat stood at my feet, fixated on something behind me. Seemingly, it tracked an unseen entity moving behind me with its eyes. Its tail tip waved menacingly, but when I turned around, I saw nothing.

Taking the candle, I circled the room. Behind the shifting curtain, the door was securely closed. The windows were closed and locked, and everywhere the silence was absolute. The cat observed my actions. I bent down and stroked its head, yet it persisted in its eerie surveillance of the room's corners.

When I returned to my divan after adding a fresh log to the fire, I felt more at ease. As a precaution – and slightly amused at my own paranoia – I positioned the fire tongs within arm's reach. Yet, the cat would not let me sleep. Eventually, I concluded it was thirsty and ventured out to find water, holding the candle without its stand. I wandered through a series of closed and vacant rooms before discovering a small bathroom adjoining a billiard room. The cat drank eagerly while I filled a glass to bring back with me. The candle emitted an unsteady light that threatened to leave me lost in the labyrinth of hallways, and gusts of wind occasionally punctuated the silence. The cat lingered by my feet, its fur standing on end. I've never been fond of cats; there's something uncanny about them.

Upon returning to the large room, I found Hotchkiss still asleep. I rearranged his boots away from the fire and adjusted the candle's wick. Sleep eluded me now, so I reclined on my divan and reflected on various matters. I thought about my foolishness in coming here, Alison West's recent presence in this house, and the growing distance between Richey and me. These thoughts led me back to Alison and the potential barrier that my modest financial situation might pose.

The sense of emptiness and silence weighed heavily on me. At one point, I heard rhythmic footsteps approaching, neither hurried nor dragging, as if they ascended endless staircases without drawing any closer. Eventually, I realized that I had not completely turned off the tap in the lavatory, which must be quite close.

The cat lay by the fire, its nose nestled between folded paws, content in the warmth and companionship. I watched it idly. Occasionally, the green wood sizzled in the fire, but the cat remained unfazed. Lightning flashed through an uncovered window. Suddenly, the cat raised its head and fixed its gaze on the gallery above. It blinked, then stared again. I was amused. Only when the cat stood up, its eyes still locked on the balcony, tail twitching at the tip and fur bristling, did I casually glance overhead.

Emerging from the shadows, a face peered down at me – a face perfectly suited to the eerie room beneath. I saw it as distinctly as I might observe my own reflection in a mirror. While I stared at it with horrified eyes, it faded away. The balcony railing remained, and the Bokhara rug still hung from it, but the gallery was empty.

The cat threw back its head and wailed mournfully.

Chapter Twenty-Four
HIS WIFE'S FATHER

I jumped up and grabbed the fire tongs. The cat's wail had woken up Hotchkiss, who immediately grasped the situation, seeing my defensive stance, the tongs and the direction of my gaze.

He grabbed the candle and dashed into the hallway, with me following closely. Up the stairs and through a small door on the right, we reached the gallery. The fire below glowed warmly, but the cat was gone. There was no sign of the ghostly figure, but as we stood there, the Bokhara rug slid over the railing and fell to the floor below.

"Man or woman?" Hotchkiss asked in his professional tone.

"Neither… I mean, I'm not sure. I only noticed the eyes," I mumbled. "That stare… You should've heard that cat, that was a classic graveyard wail."

"I doubt you saw anything," he cheerfully lied. "You dozed off, and the rest you can blame on the food in the restaurant car."

Still, he carefully examined the Bokhara rug when we went down. When I eventually dozed off, he was engrossed in the only book available, *Elwell on Bridge*. The first light of dawn was filtering into the room when he woke me, putting a finger to his lips and whispering as I struggled to put on my boots. "I think we've got him," he triumphantly declared. "I've been snooping around a bit. Right before we entered through the window last night, someone else did too. But unlike you, this person didn't drop. They swung onto the stair railing and then down. The railing's scratched. They got ahead of us enough to raid the dining room, grabbing a decanter from the sideboard. They poured a drink, left the decanter, and took the whisky to the library across the hall. Then… They broke into a desk, using a paper knife as a makeshift tool."

"Hotchkiss, it might've been Sullivan himself! He's slipping away!" I protested.

"It was Sullivan," Hotchkiss responded calmly. "And he's still here. His boots are by the library fireplace."

"He probably had a dozen pairs stashed around," I scoffed. "And while we were sitting and napping, the very man we're after was watching us from that railing."

"Easy there, my friend," Hotchkiss advised, as I slipped into my other shoe. "I didn't say he was gone. Don't rush to conclusions. It prevents clear thinking. After scaring you nearly witless, what would our gentleman naturally do? He probably took refuge upstairs, near the roof, locked himself in and went to bed.

"And he's still there?"

"Yes, he's still there."

We were unarmed. I know the typical hero always carries weapons, and Hotchkiss, being the comic relief, should have had a malfunctioning gun. In reality, we had nothing of the sort. Hotchkiss had the fire tongs, but I declined the poker.

"We just want to talk peacefully," I objected. "We can't knock him out first and have a conversation later. Plus, although I can't pinpoint it, I think your theory is shaky. If he wouldn't go to great lengths to escape us, then he's not our guy."

However, Hotchkiss was certain. He had located the room and listened to the sleeper's heavy breathing behind the door. So, we climbed past luxurious suites in the growing daylight, gasping for breath when we finally reached our destination. It was a tower room, reached by narrow stairs, well above the roofline. Hotchkiss was beaming.

"It's partly luck, but not all," he whispered, catching his breath. "If we had kept searching last night, he would have sensed it and run. Now… We've got him. Are you ready?"

He forcefully knocked on the door with the fire tongs, waiting expectantly. He was right; we heard movement inside.

"Hey! Anyone in there!" Hotchkiss shouted. "You might as well come out. We won't harm you if you cooperate."

"Tell him we're representing the law," I suggested. "That's what's usually done."

But just then, a bullet pierced the door and thudded against the tower staircase wall. We both instinctively ducked and retreated to safety.

Hotchkiss responded by banging the door with the tongs. Another bullet followed. The situation was absurd. Perhaps we should have retreated until we were better armed, but Hotchkiss had an endless well of determination, and I was equally fired up.

"Break the lock," I proposed, and Hotchkiss, positioned to the side and out of the line of fire, responded to each bullet with a forceful blow from the tongs. After a few shots, the gunfire ceased, and the door was slowly yielding. Positioned on either side of the door, we were ready for any kind of resistance. As the door swung open, Hotchkiss poised the tongs, and I stood ready to strike.

But nothing happened.

Silence.

Finally, taking the risk of losing an eye that I value greatly, I cautiously peeked around the door and into the room. There was no desperado; just a young, frightened servant sitting on the edge of her bed, wrapped in a quilt, an empty revolver at her feet.

Our retreat down the tower stairs and into the safety of the living room was a triumphant yet comical procession, reminiscent of a defeated army in retreat. Seated on the divan, I went through bouts of laughter, regaining my sanity sporadically, only to succumb to more laughter each time I glimpsed Hotchkiss' disgruntled expression.

He paced the room, tongs still in hand, a frustrated look on his face. Eventually, he halted in front of me, demanding my attention. "Once you've finished laughing," he declared with dignity, "I'd like to explain my reasoning. Do you honestly believe that the young woman upstairs left a pair of size eight boots to dry in the library last night? Or that she poured whiskey out of that decanter?"

"They've been known to do stranger things," I offered, but his stern gaze silenced me.

"Furthermore, if she was indeed the one who stared you down from the gallery railing last night, wouldn't you think that, given her… let's say, "spirited" disposition, she could have shot you full of lead?"

"I agree," I conceded. "It wasn't the type to sit by the fire, I'll give you that. But then who was it?"

Hotchkiss was convinced it had been Sullivan, but I had doubts. Why would he sneak into his own house like a thief? If he had crossed the park when we did, as seemed likely, when we did, he hadn't made any effort to use the front door. I eventually gave up pondering and decided to mend relations with the young woman in the tower.

No sounds had reached us since our grand entrance into her room. Alone this time, I approached the tower staircase with a sense of unease. Going by previous interactions, she might just throw a chair at me. I paused at the foot of the staircase and called out.

"Hello up there," I said, attempting a casual tone. "Good morning. *Wie geht es bei ihnen?*"

No response.

"*Bonjour, mademoiselle*," I tried again. This time, there was a hint of movement from above, but nothing came crashing down on me.

"We want to apologize for waking you so abruptly this morning," I continued. "You see, we wanted to talk to you, and, well, you were difficult to rouse. We're travelers, lost in these mountains, and we're hoping for some breakfast and a chance to chat."

She appeared at the door then, and I felt her gaze assessing the top of my head from above. "Is Mr. Sullivan with you?" she asked, her voice uncertain. It was her first utterance, and she seemed unsure of herself.

"No, it's just us. If you come down and take a look, you'll see that we're two harmless individuals. Our horse, that cursed beast, decided to leave us without a farewell last night, stranding us at your gate."

She visibly relaxed and descended a few steps. "Hello, I am Jennie. I was worried I might have killed someone," she admitted. "The housekeeper left yesterday, and the other maids went with her."

When she saw that I was relatively young and not the typical image of a bandit, she was considerably relieved. However, she remained wary of Hotchkiss for some reason. She managed to provide us with a meager breakfast, given the limited provisions in the house, and later, as Hotchkiss examined scratches and replaced the Bokhara rug, I engaged in conversation with her.

"Can you tell me," I inquired, "who's been in charge of the estate since Mrs. Curtis' death?"

"No one," she replied curtly.

"Has any family member visited since the accident?"

"No, sir. It was just the two of them, and some believe Mr. Sullivan might have been killed along with his sister."

"But you don't think so?"

"No, absolutely not."

"Why?"

She turned on me, suspicious. "Are you a detective?" she demanded.

"No."

"You told him to say you were representing the law."

"I'm a lawyer. Some lawyers bend the law, but I…"

She interrupted impatiently. "Are you a sheriff's officer?"

"No. Listen, Jennie, I am exactly what I claim to be. You have to trust that. I'm in a tough spot through no fault of my own. I need you to answer some questions. If you help me, I'll do what I can for you. Do you live nearby?"

Her chin quivered, her first sign of vulnerability. "My home is in Pittsburgh," she said, "and I don't have enough money to get back there. They hadn't paid any of us for two months. They didn't pay anyone."

"Alright," I responded. "I'll send you back to Pittsburgh, with a Pullman ticket, if you answer the questions I have. Agreed?"

She eagerly agreed. Outside the window, Hotchkiss was bent over, studying footprints in the driveway.

"Now," I began, "was there a Miss West staying here?"

"Yes."

"Mr. Sullivan was interested in her?"

"Yes. She was the granddaughter of a wealthy man in Pittsburgh. My aunt has been with their family for twenty years. Mrs. Curtis wanted her brother to marry Miss West."

"Do you believe he did marry her?" I struggled to contain my excitement.

"No. There were reasons…" she stopped short.

"Do you know anything about the family? Were they New Yorkers?"

"They came from somewhere in the South. Mrs. Curtis mentioned her mother was Cuban. I don't know much about them, but Mr. Sullivan had a fierce temper, despite his appearance. People think tall, blonde folks are easygoing, but I don't believe it, sir."

"How long was Miss West here?"

"Two weeks."

I debated pushing further with my questioning. Despite my precarious situation, I couldn't delve deeper into Alison West's personal matters. If she had been ensnared by opportunists, like Sullivan and his sister seemed to have been, she was hopefully out of their clutches by now. However, a realization about the incident in the Ontario car was forming in my mind: the farmhouse encounter lacked only a motive to complete the picture. Was Sullivan truly a rogue or a criminal? Was he the murderer, or was it Mrs. Conway? The age-old question: the lady or the tiger.

Jennie continued speaking. "I hope Miss West wasn't harmed?" she asked. "We all liked her. She was nothing like Mrs. Curtis."

I wanted to say that she was unlike anyone I'd ever met, but instead, I replied, "She came out with some bruises."

She glanced at my arm. "You were on the train?"

"Yes."

She waited for more questions, but when none came, she headed for the door. Just before closing it softly, she turned back.

"Mrs. Curtis is dead? You're certain?" she inquired.

"She died instantly, I believe. Her body was never recovered. But I have reasons to believe that Mr. Sullivan is alive."

"I knew it," she murmured. "I… I think he was here the night before last. That's why I went to the tower room. I think he'd kill me if he could." As far as her round, pleasant face could show, Jennie's expression was profoundly tragic. I made a swift decision and acted upon it immediately.

"You're not being entirely open with me, Jennie," I protested. "I'm going to tell you more than I have. I was on the wrecked train, in the same car as Mrs. Curtis, Miss West, and Mr. Sullivan. During the night, a crime occurred in that car, and Mr. Sullivan vanished. But he left behind a trail of evidence that incriminated me completely, making me a potential target for arrest."

It took a moment for her to grasp the situation. Then, as the weight of my words sunk in, she looked up and gasped, "You mean… Mr. Sullivan committed the crime himself?"

"I believe he did."

"What was it?"

"It was murder," I stated plainly.

Her hands involuntarily clenched, and she recoiled. "A woman?" She could hardly form the words.

"No, a man, Mr. Simon Harrington, from Pittsburgh."

Her struggle to maintain her composure was heartbreaking. Eventually, she broke down, crying with her head resting on the back of a tall chair.

"It was my fault," she lamented, "all my fault. I shouldn't have sent them the message."

After a few moments, she regained her composure. She seemed to hesitate over something, finally deciding to reveal it.

"You'll understand better, sir, when I tell you that I was raised in the Harrington family. Mr. Harrington was Mr. Sullivan's wife's father!"

Chapter Twenty-Five
AT THE STATION

So, it had turned out to be the tiger, not the lady! Well, I had held to that theory all through. Jennie had suddenly become a valuable asset; if needed, she could establish the link between Sullivan and the murdered man, providing a motive for the crime. I was elated when Hotchkiss entered the room. When Jennie produced a photograph of Mrs. Sullivan, and I recognized the woman with bronze hair from the train, both Hotchkiss and I were satisfied. It just goes to show how fleeting most human contentments can be.

Jennie either had no further information to share or was wary of revealing too much, particularly in front of Hotchkiss. I informed her that Mrs. Sullivan was recovering in a Baltimore hospital, but she seemed to have already learned this from some other source, merely nodding in acknowledgment. After making her preparations, she left with the town's carriage, the cat in her arms. I accompanied her, and during the ride down, she shared a little more with me.

"If you happen to see Mrs. Sullivan," she advised, "and if she's conscious, she likely believes that both her husband and father were killed in the accident. She'll be in a bad state, sir."

"Are you saying she still cares about her husband?"

The cat shifted onto my lap, rubbing its head against my hand. Jennie gazed at the mountain crests, a majestic sun against a boundless sky. "Yes, she cares," she said softly. "Women are like that. They say they're like cats, but Peter here wouldn't come back to lick your hand if you kicked him. If... if you have to tell her the truth, please be as gentle as possible, sir. She's been kind to me, and that's why I've been playing the role of a spy here all summer. It's a thankless task, spying on people."

"It certainly is," I solemnly agreed.

Hotchkiss and I returned to Washington late that evening. To avoid disturbing the household, I decided to go to the club. I was at the office early the next morning and let myself in. McKnight rarely showed up before ten-thirty, and our small office staff arrived after nine. I went through the mail from the previous day and waited as patiently as I could for McKnight.

During the wait, I called Mrs. Klopton and informed her that I would be dining at home that night. The food my household manages to scrape together during my frequent absences remains a mystery to me. It's probably tea and crackers. Despite my attempts to find something more substantial, the times I arrived in the middle of the night, I've never found more than that. Perhaps it's just my imagination, but the news of an impending trip seems to cast a gloomy aura over the entire house as though Euphemia and Eliza, and Thomas, the stableman, were already surviving, in imagination, on Mrs. Klopton's meager fare.

Anyway, I rang her up and told her I was coming. Her voice sounded odd, like she was angry or something. Her voice hurt my ear through the phone. "I got a new butcher, Mr. Lawrence," she said importantly. "Last time, the roast was short by a pound, and those mutton-chops – any self-respecting sheep wouldn't acknowledge them."

I've learned that Mrs. Klopton's tone can be very revealing. I also learned how to get her to the point quickly. "Seems like you're not in a great mood this morning," I said. "What's up, Mrs. Klopton? You haven't used that tone since Euphemia baked that pie for the iceman. What happened now? Someone poisoned the dog?"

She cleared her throat. "The house got broken into, Mr. Lawrence," she said. "I've been around the best families, and I've never seen what I saw yesterday – every drawer opened, and my most precious things..." she choked.

"Did you call the police?" I asked quickly.

"Police!" she snorted. "It was the police that did it – two detectives with a warrant. I can't even tell you what one of them said when they found the whisky and rock candy for my cough."

"Did they take anything?" I snapped, on edge.

"They took the cough syrup," she said indignantly, "and they said..."

"Forget the cough syrup!" I was panicking. "Did they take anything else? Were they in my dressing room?"

"Yes. I threatened to sue, and I told them what you'd do when you got back. But they ignored me. They took that black sealskin bag you brought from Pittsburgh!"

I knew my time was running out. I had planned to find Sullivan and produce the bag (*minus* the bit of chain) as evidence against him, but now the police had it, and I was no closer to finding Sullivan than before. Hotchkiss believed he had his man in the house off Washington Circle, but Jennie said Sullivan tried to get into the Laurels that very night. What if we found Sullivan and proved the bag was his? The police had the bit of chain… and that meant involving Alison. I sat down, hiding my face in my hands. I realized that there was no way out.

Against me was the evidence of the survivors of the Ontario that I had been accused of the murder at the time. There were bloodstains on my pillow and a hidden dagger. Plus, they found in my possession a bag with the dead guy's wallet.

In my favor was McKnight's theory against Mrs. Conway. She had a motive for wanting the notes, she thought I was in lower ten, and collapsed when the crime was discovered in the morning.

Against both these theories, I accused a purely imaginary person named Sullivan, who no survivor except Alison had seen – and I couldn't involve her. I could find a motive for his murdering his despised father-in-law, but that, again, would bring the girl into the case.

And none of the theories explained the telegram and the broken necklace.

Outside, the office staff was arriving, blissfully unaware of my presence. Snippets of conversation and the stenographer's laughter drifted over the transom. McKnight's relative, a law student who used breaks to call young women, came in singing, and the fifteen-year old office boy, Blobs, joined in. I smiled grimly, too preoccupied with my own troubles to enjoy startling them into silence by opening the door. I even heard, without resentment, Blobs asking when "Blake" would return.

I hoped McKnight would show up before the arrest occurred. There were many things to sort out. But when I finally called him, I found he'd been gone for over an hour. It was clear he wasn't headed straight to the office. With what little resignation I could muster, I paced and waited.

I felt more alone than ever. As Richey said, being "born an orphan," I'd forged my own path and achieved my success. I'd built my life on the pillars of law and order, and now an unknown force had pulled away the pillars, leaving me amidst ruins.

Perhaps it's the maternal aspect in a woman that makes a man turn to her when all else fails. His inner child seeks to have his wounded pride soothed, his frayed self-esteem mended. If he loves her, he wants her to kiss the pain away.

My longing to see Alison, a constant presence, overwhelmed me that morning. I thought I might not see her again. I had little to say except one thing, which I hesitated to utter under the cloud hanging over me. Yet I yearned to see her, to feel her touch – the way only a lonely man can crave. I sought her comfort, the solace that came from her mere presence. So, with each step outside my refuge a looming threat, I dialed her number.

She was gone! I felt deeply disappointed. They told me she was heading home to Richmond, but there was a chance to catch her at the station.

Seeing her had become an overwhelming need, so, oblivious of the shock my sudden appearance would bring to the office, I grabbed my hat, swung open the door, and dashed to the elevator. I caught a glimpse of Johnson and two others going up in the next elevator as I descended, but I hardly registered them. No horse-drawn cab was in sight, so I hopped onto a passing streetcar. I didn't care about the consequences – arrest, jail, disgrace – I was determined to see Alison.

And I did see her. When I burst into the station, she wasn't there. I hurried back to the gates, and there she was – dressed in the familiar blue gown I always associated with her, the same one she had worn when, in a moment of weakness, I had kissed her at the Carter farm. But she wasn't alone. Richey was there, leaning in, speaking earnestly with all his devotion written on his face.

They didn't notice me, and I was relieved. After all, McKnight had the precedence over me. I turned on my heel and walked out of the station in a daze. I glanced back once before they vanished from view, standing there, engrossed in each other, the only two people in the world I cared about. I left them together and returned to the office, bracing myself for the impending arrest.

Chapter Twenty-Six
ON TO RICHMOND

THE PURLOINED LETTER – "The Purloined Letter" is a short story by Edgar Allan Poe and the third of his three detective stories featuring C. Auguste Dupin.

Oddly, nothing disturbed me that day. McKnight was conspicuously absent. I spent the afternoon at my desk, carrying out routine tasks with feverish intensity. Like someone on the brink of a serious illness or a perilous journey, I cleared my correspondence, signed checks until my hand cramped, reviewed my will, and paid my life insurance, to the benefit of my elderly maternal aunt. I no longer dreaded my arrest. After the incident at the station that morning, I welcomed any change from the tension. Returning home openly, I invited the warrant I knew was waiting, yet no one accosted me. The delay puzzled me.

The evening passed uneventfully. I read until late, occasionally pausing as my book lay beside me, lost in thought while I smoked. Mrs. Klopton meticulously secured ostentatiously the house around eleven and lingered, eager to share her outrage about the police search. I didn't encourage her.

"In all honesty," she pompously concluded, one foot in the hall, "one might think, Mr. Lawrence, you were involved in something untoward. They behaved as though you had committed a crime."

"Frankly, Mrs. Klopton," I said wearily, "I'm not entirely sure I haven't. Given the prevailing opinion, all seems to point in my direction."

She stared at me in shocked silence before storming out. She returned briefly to inform me that the paper predicted cooler weather and she had put an extra blanket on my bed. Much to her disappointment, I declined to reopen the subject.

At half past eleven, McKnight and Hotchkiss arrived. Richey has a habit of pulling up in front of the house and honking until someone appeared. He has a complex horn code that I can never remember. Two long and one short honks mean something like "Bring out a box of cigarettes," while six short honks resembling a police call translate to "Can you lend me some money?" Tonight, it was evident something was afoot as he just stepped out and rang the doorbell.

They entered the library, and Hotchkiss polished his collar until it gleamed. McKnight was exuberantly cheerful. "Still a free man!" he exclaimed. "Can you believe your luck? You've always been a fortunate devil, Lawrence."

"Yes," I agreed with a tinge of bitterness, "Sometimes I can barely contain my delight. By the way, Hotchkiss, did you know that the police were here while we were at Cresson? They found the bag I brought from the wreck."

"We're reaching a crucial point," he mused, "unless a certain plan of mine…" he hesitated.

"I hope so. I'm pretty desperate," I admitted. "I've got a sort of mental toothache, the sooner it's pulled the better."

"Don't worry," McKnight reassured me. "Imagine the firm's shame if the senior partner ends up doing life or worse…" He mimed a noose with his handkerchief. "Prison isn't all bad," he continued. "Some folks keep going back." He glanced at his watch, his cheerfulness strained. Hotchkiss was nervously fumbling my book. "Did you read "The Purloined Letter," Mr. Blakeley?" he asked.

"Probably, years ago. Poe, right?" I recalled.

He was baffled by my indifference. "It is a masterpiece," he enthused. "Read it again today."

"So, what's the scoop?"

"I checked out the rooms near Washington Circle. Found out a few things, Mr. Blakeley. First of all, our guy's left-handed." he looked around for our approval. "There was a small cushion on the dresser, and the scarf pins in it had been stuck in with the left hand."

"Could've been twisted by someone," I countered, but I backed down, as he looked hurt.

"There's only one discrepancy," he admitted, worried, "but it bothers me. Mrs. Carter said our man wore flashy pajamas, while I found the plainest nightshirts."

"Any buttons missing?" McKnight glanced at his watch again.

"The buttons were there," said the amateur detective seriously. "But the buttonhole next to the top one was torn."

McKnight slyly winked at me.

"I'm certain about one thing," Hotchkiss continued, clearing his throat. "The papers aren't in that room. He either has them on him or he's sold them."

A noise on the street made my visitors listen intently. It passed on, though. I was getting curious and McKnight was struggling to contain himself. Secrecy isn't his strong suit. During the pause, we talked about the odd event at Cresson, which lost nothing by Hotchkiss' dry narration.

"So," he concluded, "the woman in the Baltimore hospital is Henry Sullivan's wife and the daughter of the man he murdered. No wonder he collapsed when he heard about the wreck."

"Probably overwhelmed by joy," McKnight added. "Is that clock right, Lawrence? Actually, never mind. By the way, Mrs. Conway swung by the office yesterday while you were out."

"What!" I jumped up from my chair.

"Yep. She mentioned she'd heard good things about us and wanted our help with her case against the railroad."

"I'm curious about her intentions," I pondered. "Is she trying to reach me through you?"

Richey's casual demeanor often hides deeper emotions. He dropped the act now. "Yes," he said, "she's after the notes, of course. I felt pretty lousy when I turned her down. She stood by the door, looking pale, and told me scornfully that I could save you from a murder charge but chose not to. I felt like a coward. I was as guilty as if I could've helped her. She hinted that there were reasons and she blamed my stance on some rotten motives."

"Nonsense," I replied as calmly as I could. Hotchkiss had gone to the window. "She was worked up. There are no 'reasons,' whatever she's talking about."

Richey patted my shoulder. "We've been through too much to let any 'reasons' or 'unreasons' come between us, buddy," he said, not very steadily.

Hotchkiss, who had been silent, now approached with his most imposing demeanor. He put his hands under his coat-tails and coughed. "Mr. Blakeley," he began, "following Mr. McKnight's suggestion, we've arranged a little meeting here tonight. If all went as planned, Henry Pinckney Sullivan is probably under arrest by now. Very shortly, he should be here."

"I wanted to chat with him before he got locked up," Richey explained. "He's smart enough to be interesting, and honestly, I'm not as sure about his guilt as our friend the 'very small cog in the government's machinery.' No respectable murderer needs six different motives for the same crime, ranging from robbery to a difficult father-in-law."

We fell into silence. McKnight positioned himself at a window, and Hotchkiss paced the floor expectantly. "It's a great day for modern detective methods," he chirped. "While the cops were guarding houses and waiting for clues to fall into their laps, we've been assembling piece by piece a puzzle..."

The doorbell rang, followed swiftly by footsteps in the hallway. McKnight swung the door open, and Hotchkiss, standing on his toes, gestured dramatically. "Here's our man," he proclaimed.

Through the doorway strolled a tall, blond guy dressed in light gray, sporting tan shoes, and escorted closely by a police officer.

"I brought him here like you suggested, Mr. McKnight," the constable reported.

But McKnight was bent over the library table, laughing silently, and I wasn't much better. Hotchkiss now looked crestfallen, while the blond man shifted from anger to embarrassment. It was Stuart, our confidential clerk for the past six years!

McKnight sat up and wiped his eyes. "Stuart," he said sternly, "there are two very serious things we've discovered about you. First, you stab your scarf pins into your cushion with your left hand, which is quite unacceptable. Second, you wear, uh, night-shirts instead of pajamas. Worse than that, we've found one with a torn buttonhole at the neck."

Stuart looked baffled. He glanced from McKnight to me, then at the dejected Hotchkiss.

"I have no clue what's going on," he said. "I was arrested when I got back to my boarding house tonight after the theater, and brought straight here. I told the officer it was a mistake."

Poor Hotchkiss made a brave attempt to justify the fiasco. "You can't deny," he argued, "that Mr. Andrew Bronson followed you to your rooms last Monday evening."

Stuart looked at us and blushed. "No, I won't deny it," he said, "but there was nothing criminal about it, at least on my part. Mr. Bronson has been trying to convince me to get the forged notes for him. But I didn't even know where they were."

"And you weren't on the wrecked Washington Flier?" Hotchkiss persisted.

But McKnight intervened. "It's pointless trying to put the other man's identity on Stuart, Mr. Hotchkiss," he objected. "He's been our confidential clerk for six years, and he hasn't taken a day off in a year. I'm afraid the intricate story we've woven from these scraps of evidence is turning into a crazy quilt." His tone was lighthearted, but I could sense a hint of genuine disappointment.

I paid the constable for his trouble, and he left. Stuart, still irritated, left to go back to Washington Circle. He shook hands with McKnight and me in a magnanimous manner but cast a look of pure animosity at Hotchkiss, who was still slumped in his chair.

"As far as I can tell," McKnight remarked dryly, "we're in exactly the same spot as when we met at the Carter place. We're no closer to finding our man."

"We might have one valuable lead," I suggested. "He's the husband of a woman with bronze hair at Van Kirk's hospital. Maybe we can track him through her. Mr. Hotchkiss, I hope we're not losing your valuable assistance?"

He perked up a bit at that. "Oh, no, of course not, if you still want me. I was just thinking about the man who left, Stuart, right? I told his landlady tonight that he wouldn't be needing the room anymore. I hope she hasn't rented it out already."

We tried to lift his spirits as best we could. I proposed that we head to Baltimore the next day to locate the real Sullivan through his wife. He departed sometime after midnight, leaving Richey and me alone.

He pulled a chair close to the lamp, lit a cigarette, and we sat in silence for a while. I stayed in the shadows, observing him. It wasn't surprising, I thought, that she had feelings for him. Women always seemed to love him, perhaps because he always reciprocated. It wasn't disloyal to think that; it was simply his nature to give and seek affection. However, I was different. I had never cared deeply for a girl before, and my life had been devoid of love. I had always fought my battles alone. There was a time in college when we both vied for the attention of the same girl. Her name was Dorothy, I forgot her last name. But I remember very well that I had, in an act of youthful nobility, stepped aside for Richey and had moved on without resentment, embracing a self-imposed, intense martyrdom. As is often the case, our trains of thought intersected.

"Hey, Lollie," he began, "do you remember Dorothy Browne?"

Browne, that was it! "Dorothy Browne? Oh, yes, I remember her. Why do you ask?"

"Nothing," he replied. "I was just thinking about her. That's all. You remember how infatuated you were with her and how you backed off when she chose me?"

"I stepped aside," I asserted with dignity, "because you claimed you'd shoot yourself if she didn't accompany you to some event or another!"

"Ah, yes, I recall that now." he tossed his cigarette toward the fireplace and rose. There was a subtle self-awareness between us, and he positioned himself with his back to me, idly handling a Japanese vase on the mantel.

"I was considering," he began, adjusting the vase, "that if you're feeling better and ready to dive back in, I'd like to take a week off or so. The office is in pretty good shape."

"Are you saying you're heading to Richmond?" I inquired after a barely noticeable pause. He turned to face me, hands in his pockets.

"No. That's off, Lollie. The Seiberts are planning a week-long coastal cruise. The heat has taken a toll on me, and the cruise promises seven days of fresh air and bridge."

I lit a cigarette and extended the box to him, but he declined. Fatigue and weariness were etched on his face. Neither of us seemed to find the right words, and the matter between us ran too deep for conversation.

"How's Candida?" he inquired.

"Martin says she'll be fine in a month," I responded in a similar manner.

He grabbed his hat, but he had more to add. He blurted it out as he was halfway to the door. "The Seiberts aren't leaving for a couple of days," he mentioned. "If you want a day or so off to go down to Richmond yourself…"

"Maybe I will," I replied with feigned indifference. "You're not leaving right away, are you?"

"Yes, it's getting late." He inhaled as if he wanted to say more, but the moment passed. "Well, good night," he called from the doorway.

"Good night, my friend."

In the next instant, the outer door slammed shut, and then the hum of the Cannonball's engine echoed in the street. The quiet settled around me again, and there, bathed in lamplight, I indulged in my dreams. I was going to see her.

Suddenly, the thought of being shut away, even temporarily, from a world so grand and wonderful became unbearable. The prospect of getting arrested before reaching Richmond was nightmarish, an endless ordeal. The next morning, I sneaked out of the house through the stable entrance and navigated a maze of dark paths to reach the office. There, following a meeting with Blobs, whose excitement was palpable in his twitchy features, I locked my private office door and tackled some urgent tasks. By ten o'clock I was free, and I double checked my train schedule. At five minutes past ten, with no sign of McKnight, Blobs knocked on the door, using the double rap we had agreed upon. I let him in, and he closed the door quietly behind him. His eyes sparkled with enthusiasm, and a smudge of purple typewriter ink gave him a strangely villainous look.

"They're here," he whispered, "two of them, and that crazy Stuart wasn't on, and he mentioned you were somewhere in the building."

A door slammed outside, and footsteps echoed in the uncarpeted outer office.

"This way," Blobs murmured in a husky voice. He swiftly entered a restroom, unlocking a door I had always assumed was sealed. We proceeded through a back hallway stacked with boxes and past the printing presses of a bookbindery to a freight elevator.

To Blobs' disappointment, there was no pursuit. I was exhilarated but out of breath when we emerged into an alley, the bright daylight shining on Blobs' excited face.

"Quite the adventure, huh?" I gasped, slipping a dollar into his hand.

"Give me two more dollars, and I'll drop them down the elevator shaft," he suggested with a fierce grin. I left him there with his bloodthirsty plans and headed to the station. I occasionally glanced over my shoulder, but I managed to reach the station unnoticed. The afternoon was hot, and the train moved sluggishly, pausing at sweltering stations where the heat seemed to rise in waves from their roofs. Yet I

observed these things with detachment, as my destination held a girl
with blue eyes and dark brown hair. Hair that could – hadn't I seen it? –
fall in enchanting tangles or be artfully coiled into charming knots.

Chapter Twenty-Seven
THE SEA, THE SAND, THE STARS

- NOTES -

TIMEO DANAOS – "Timeo Danaos et dona ferentes" ("I fear the Greeks even when bearing gifts") is a Latin phrase from the Aeneid, *a Latin epic poem written by Virgil. The phrase is spoken by Trojan priest Laocoön referring to the famous Trojan Horse left by the Greeks as a parting gift when they pretended to give up the siege of Troy and return to their lands in defeat. This expression is used to suggest that you shouldn't trust your enemies, even (or especially!) when they are acting too friendly.*

"LITTLE GOAT BLEAT: LITTLE TABLE APPEAR!" – This quote comes from the German fairy tale entitled "One-Eye, Two-Eyes, and Three-Eyes," collected by the Brothers Grimm. In this fairy tale, a wise woman, taking pity on a hungry little girl called 'Little Two-eyes', says to her: "Dry your eyes, and I will tell you something so that you need never be hungry again. Only say to your goat,
'Little goat, bleat,
Little table, appear,'
and a beautifully spread table will stand before you, with the most delicious food on it, so that you can eat as much as you want. And when you have had enough and don't want the little table any more, you have only to say,
'Little goat, bleat,
Little table, away,"
and then it will vanish.'"

IF SEVEN MAIDS WITH SEVEN MOPS SWEPT IT FOR HALF A YEAR, DO YOU SUPPOSE, THE WALRUS SAID, THAT THEY COULD GET IT CLEAR? – This quote is from the poem "The Walrus and the Carpenter" by Lewis Carroll which appears in Through the Looking Glass and What Alice Found There. *The walrus in the poem thinks a beach would be much better without sand is wondering if it could be cleared away.*

I called right after checking into my hotel, feeling a rush of anticipation to see her. Turns out, she was out of town. Disappointment hit me like a wave when I hung up the phone. It took me a few minutes to consider calling again and asking if she was reachable by phone. She was down by the bay with the Samuel Forbeses.

Sammy Forbes! I remembered that name. Back in college, I hadn't thought much of him, but now I was open to embracing him. He had always meant well, and he had a reputation for being generously spontaneous. So, I gave him a call.

"By Jove!" he exclaimed upon hearing my voice. "Blakeley, the Fount of Wisdom against Woman! Blakeley, the Great Unkissed! Welcome to our city!"

He invited me to join him at the Shack, describing me as a pleasant surprise. Apparently, multiple guys had called within hours, inquiring if Alison West was staying with him and subtly hinting at their availability.

"Oh, Miss West!" I replied politely, though I sensed a faint buzz on the line. "Is she there?" Sam remained unsuspecting, continuing to see me as the Great Unkissed. He promptly invited me over, brushing aside my protests.

"Don't be silly," he dismissed my objections. "Come on down. The lady who runs my boarding-house is practically demanding it. Remember Dorothy, right? Dorothy Browne? She's convinced that you can wear my clothes just fine, unless you've lost your shape. All you need here is a swimsuit for the day and a dinner jacket for the evening."

"It sounds tempting," I hesitated. "If you're sure it's not a bother… alright, Sam, since you and your wife are kind enough. I have a couple of free days. Give my regards to Dorothy until I can do it myself."

Sam greeted me in person and chauffeured me to the Shack, a grand house with a waterfront view. Along the way, he shared that many married men believed they were content, but were merely resigned. However, he extolled the virtues of his chosen lifestyle and proudly mentioned that Sam Junior was a great swimmer. He also mentioned that Alison was his wife's cousin, their grandmothers having both married the same man at different times. According to Sam, Alison would lose her looks if she wasn't careful.

"I'm convinced she's troubled," he asserted, as he handed the reins to a stable hand and prepared to exit the carriage. "You know her, and she's the type you think you understand completely. But you don't; don't kid yourself. Observe her closely at dinner, Blake; you won't become infatuated like the other guys… Tell me what's going on with her. We really care about Allie."

He lumbered up the steps, heavier than when I last knew him. At the door, he paused. "Do you know the MacLures at Seal Harbor?" he asked oddly. Just then, the lady of the house entered the hallway, extending a warm welcome with both hands. Whatever Forbes had intended to discuss, he didn't bring it up again.

"We're having tea in here," Dorothy exclaimed cheerfully, motioning to the door behind her. "Tea, sort of, since it's the only beverage missing. Then we'll get dressed for hop night at the club."

"Which is as much a misnomer as the tea," Sam chimed in, laboriously shedding his linen driving coat. "It's bridge night, and the only hops are in the beer."

He continued chuckling about this as he led me upstairs. He showed me my room and then embarked on a fruitless search for suitable evening attire. I ended up skipping the club that night because I couldn't fit into Sam's clothes. That became abundantly clear after a sweaty half-hour struggle.

"I can't do it, Sam," I said, draping his formal coat over me like a toga. "Who am I to have excess clothing when many don't even have enough? I won't do it. I'm selfish, but not that selfish."

"Good Lord," he exclaimed, wiping his forehead. "You've maintained your figure! I can't wear a belt anymore; it's suspenders for me."

He ruminated on his predicament, perched on the edge of the bed. "You *could* go as you are," he finally suggested. "We do it all the time, but tonight happens to be a special event, and…," his words trailed off as he struggled to buckle my belt around him. "About six inches too tight," he sighed. "I expect horses to take flight when I step into a hansom cab. Well, Allie isn't going either. She turned down Granger this afternoon, the guy from Annapolis you met on the stairs… thin fellow. And she always claims a headache on those occasions."

He heaved himself up and headed toward the door. "Granger is leaving," he mentioned. "I might be able to borrow his dinner coat for you. How well do you know her?" he inquired, hand on the doorknob.

"You mean Dolly…?"

"Alison."

"Fairly well," I answered cautiously. "Not as well as I'd like. I had dinner with her in Washington last week. And… we have some history before that."

Forbes rang the bell instead of going out, and asked the servant who appeared to check if Mr. Granger's suitcase was gone. If not, he asked for it to be brought across the hall. Then he returned to his perch on the bed.

"We feel responsible for Allie, you know… close family and all that," he began with an air of importance. "We can't talk to the people here at the house, every guy's smitten with her, and the women are green-eyed. Plus, there's a lot of money, or there will be."

"Damn the money," I muttered, almost cutting myself. "Sorry, the razor slipped."

"I can tell you," he continued, "because you're not easily swayed by every pretty face… though Allie is more than just that, of course. About a month ago, she left to visit Janet MacLure at Seal Harbor. You know her? She returned to Richmond yesterday and then came here… Allie, that is. Yesterday afternoon, Dolly received a letter from Janet, something about a second man and how she wished Alison had been there, as she had promised them a two-week visit! What do you make of that? And that's not even the worst part. Allie wasn't in the room, but there were eight other women there. Dolly had used belladonna in her eyes the night before to see how she'd look, and as a result, she couldn't see anything closer than across the room. So, someone read the letter out loud, and the entire story spilled out. One of the girls blabbed to Granger, and today the fellow proposed to Allie to show her he couldn't care less about where she'd been."

"Good for him!" I chimed in, genuinely pleased. I had a liking for Granger, now that he was out of the competition. However, Sam regarded me suspiciously.

"Blake," he remarked, "if I didn't know you so well, I'd think you were interested in her yourself."

Being so close to her, under the same roof, with the weight of a clandestine secret between us, was making me dizzy. I nudged Forbes toward the door. "Me, interested?" I scoffed, holding onto his shoulders. "There's no word in your vocabulary to describe my state.

I'm an island floating in a sea of emotions, Sam… An empty place surrounded by longing, a…"

"An empty place surrounded by longing?!" he interrupted. "You want your dinner, that's what's wrong with you…"

I shut the door on him then. He suddenly seemed mundane. Dinner, I thought! Though, as a matter of fact, I managed a decent meal later on, wearing Granger's coat and someone else's trousers, since Granger's suitcase hadn't been taken away.

Alison didn't appear for dinner, confirming she wouldn't be heading to the club-house dance. I used my injured arm and a fictitious, vaguely described sprain from the accident as excuses to stay home. Sam entertained the table with stories of my skepticism toward women, and my one love affair… with Dorothy. I responded as expected, admitting that only my failure there had kept me single all these years. I joked about comforting his distraught widow when Sam mysteriously disappears without a trace while swimming tomorrow and so on.

After the never-ending meal, after yards of white veils covering pounds of hair and about eight outfits with their accompanying accessories had been stuffed into three cars and a trap, I took a deep breath and turned around. At that moment, I had just one goal in mind: To find Alison, assure her of my unwavering confidence in her, and offer my assistance and myself, if she'd have me, in her service.

Finding her proved to be a challenge. I combed through the lower level, the verandas, and the grounds with caution. Eventually, I encountered a young English girl who turned out to be her maid. She was also on the search, worried because her mistress hadn't had dinner, and the tray of food she carried was rapidly cooling. I relieved her of the tray, having spotted something white along the shore. And that's when I crossed paths with the Girl again.

Seated on an upturned boat, her chin resting on her hands, she gazed out at the sea. The gentle tide of the bay nearly touched her feet, and the drapery of her white dress blended hazily with the sands. She resembled a specter, a melancholic phantom of the sea, although the adjective is somewhat redundant – cheerful phantoms are unheard of, after all.

Oddly, given her apparent sorrow, she was softly whistling to herself, a mournful minor melody. She glanced up swiftly as I stumbled, causing the dishes on the tray to clink. All things considered, the tray didn't quite fit into the scene: the sea, the misty starlight, the girl with her beauty – even the melancholy little tune that paused now and then before resuming, as if it fought against a trembling lip. And then I arrived, accompanied by a tray of dainty silver dishes, jingling and carrying the unmistakable aroma of broiled chicken!

"Oh!" she exclaimed, and then, "Oh! I thought you were Jenkins."

"*Timeo Danaos…* what's the rest of it?" I quipped, offering the tray. "You missed dinner, you know." I settled beside her. "Look, I'll be the table. Remember that old fairy tale? 'Little goat bleat: little table appear!' I'm willing to be the goat, too."

She chuckled, a slightly shaky laughter.

"We never seem to encounter each other like normal people, do we?" she mused. "We should probably shake hands and ask 'how do you do.'"

"I don't want to meet you like normal people. And I suppose you always picture me in someone else's clothes," I replied modestly. "I'm doing it again, can't seem to help myself. These are Granger's clothes I'm wearing now."

She tilted her head back and laughed once more, this time with genuine delight.

"It's just so ridiculous," she said, "and you've only ever seen me while I'm eating!"

"Speaking of which, the chicken's cooling off while the ice is warming up," I pointed out. "At the time, I thought there was no better place than the farmhouse kitchen for this, but I've changed my mind. I arranged all this for something I want to share with you – the sea, the sand, the stars."

"How poetic you are with your alliteration!" she remarked, trying to sound playful. "But you're not allowed to say anything until I've had my supper. Look at how everything's scattered around!"

However, she ended up not eating anything, and before long, I set the tray down on the sand. We didn't feel rushed; time seemed irrelevant against the timeless rhythm of the sea. The breeze tousled her hair into small damp curls against her face, and gradually, the tide withdrew, leaving our boat as an island in a sea of gray sand.

"*If seven maids with seven mops swept it for half a year, Do you suppose, the walrus said, that they could get it clear?*" she quipped at me, once she realized that I was about to say something.

I held her hand, and as long as I simply held it, she allowed it to rest warmly in mine. But when I brought it to my lips and planted a kiss on her soft, open palm, she gently withdrew it, without any sign of displeasure.

"Not that, please," she protested, then resumed her soft whistling, her chin propped up by her hands. "I can't sing," she explained, breaking an awkward silence, "so, when I'm restless or have something on my mind, I whistle. I hope you don't mind?"

"I love it," I declared fervently. I did; whenever she puckered her lips like that, I wanted to kiss them.

"I saw you… at the station," she suddenly mentioned. "You seemed eager to leave."

I remained silent, and after a pause, she let out a deep breath. "Men are peculiar creatures, aren't they?" she said and resumed her whistling. After a while, she sat up as if she'd reached a decision. "I'm going to confess something," she announced out of the blue. "You mentioned, you know, that you'd arranged all this because there was something you wanted to tell me. But the truth is, *I* arranged it all – I came here, I mean – because I knew you'd come, and I had something to tell you. Something so miserable that I needed this setting to help me get through it."

"I don't want to hear anything that causes you distress to say," I reassured her. "I didn't come here to pry into your secrets, Alison. I came because I couldn't resist it." She didn't object to my use of her name.

"Have you found… your documents?" she asked, looking directly into my eyes, perhaps for the first time.

"Not yet. We're still hoping," I replied.

"Have the authorities bothered you?" she inquired.

"They haven't had any opportunity," I equivocated. "You needn't distress yourself about that, anyhow."

"But I do wonder why you still believe in me when nobody else does," she murmured.

"I wonder," I echoed, "why I do."

"If you can produce Harry Sullivan," she mused aloud, "and if you can establish a connection between him and Mr. Bronson, and uncover the full story of why he was on that train, would it help?"

I acknowledged that it would. Now that the whole truth was almost within reach, I felt a familiar fear creeping in. I didn't want to hear what she might reveal. The broken line of gold on the horizon, where the moon was rising, resembled a fractured chain of glistening links. My heel in the sand felt was once again was pressing on a woman's tender fingers. I jolted myself back to reality.

"For your revelations to be helpful, perhaps you would need to share them with the police," I said cautiously, "especially now that they have discovered the missing end of the necklace…"

"The end of the necklace," she repeated, her voice hollow. "What about the end of the necklace?"

I stared at her. "Don't you remember the end of the cameo necklace, the part that had broken off and was found in the black sealskin bag, stained with… well, with blood?"

"Blood," she murmured. "So you found the broken end? And then… you had my gold purse, and you saw the necklace inside it, and you… you must have assumed…"

"I didn't assume anything," I hastened to clarify. "Alison, I never thought anything other than the fact that you were troubled, and that I had no right to intrude. Believe me, I thought you didn't want my help."

She extended her hand, and I enveloped it with both of mine. There had been no declarations of love between us, yet it felt like she knew and understood. It was one of those rare moments that occur infrequently in life, usually only during great crises, an instance of complete understanding and trust.

She withdrew her hand and sat up, resolute and unwavering, her fingers interlaced in her lap. As she spoke, the moon ascended leisurely, casting a radiant path across the water. In the trees behind us a sleepy bird let out a drowsy chirp, and a wave, more assertive than the others, swept up the sand, bringing the moon's silvery touch to our very feet.

I bent toward her. "I have just one question," I said.

"Ask away," she responded, her voice tinged with weariness. "Whatever you like."

"Was it something related to the information you're about to share that made you refuse Richey?" I inquired.

She inhaled sharply. "No," she answered, without looking at me. "No, that wasn't the reason."

Chapter Twenty-Eight
ALISON'S STORY

She told her story evenly, her gaze fixed on the water. Occasionally,
when I too looked seaward, I thought she gave me secretive glances.
Once, she paused in the midst of it all.

"You might not realize it," she protested, "but you come across like a
war god. Your face is terrifying."

"I'll turn away if that helps," I responded with frustration, "but don't
expect me to look anything but furious. You can't fathom what I'm
going through."

The story of her encounter with the Curtis woman was succinct. They
initially met in Rome, where Alison and her mother rented a villa for a
year. Mrs. Curtis skirted the fringes of society there, pleading post-war
poverty as an excuse for not going out more. There were rumors about
a brother, although Alison hadn't seen him. After a scandal involving
Mrs. Curtis and a young attaché from the Austrian embassy, Alison was
forbidden from associating with her.

"The women never really liked her," she said. "She did
unconventional things, and that didn't fly well in the conventional
circles there. They also said she sometimes left gambling debts unpaid. I
didn't really care for those people. I believed their dislike stemmed
from her being poor yet popular. Then, we returned home, and I
almost forgot about her. But last spring, when mother wasn't well – she
had taken grandfather to the Riviera, which always drains her – we went
to Virginia Hot Springs. We met her and her brother there, Harry
Pinckney Sullivan."

"I know. Keep going."

"Mother had a nurse, and I had a lot of time on my own. They were quite friendly to me. I saw them frequently. The brother intrigued me, partly because he didn't flirt with me. He almost seemed to avoid me, which piqued my interest. I suppose I had been spoiled. Most other men I knew had… well, you know."

"I'm aware of that too," I said harshly, distancing myself from her slightly. I was cruel, but the entire story was agonizing. I think she understood my suffering because she didn't show any resentment.

"It was early in the season, and not many people were around. None that I cared about. Mother and the nurse were obsessed with cribbage, and it felt like those little pegs were being driven into my head. When Mrs. Curtis arranged outings and picnics, I… well, I sneaked away and joined them. You probably won't believe me, but I hadn't done that kind of thing before. Well, I guess I've paid for it now."

"What did Sullivan look like?" I pressed, pacing on the sand. I remember angrily kicking at a water-soaked board in my path.

"Very handsome. Tall like you, but fair and even more straight."

My shoulders tensed. I am straight enough, but I was sagging with seething jealousy.

"When my mother got better, someone informed her about my association with Mrs. Curtis and her brother. We had a terrible fight, and I was hauled home like a misbehaving child. Did anybody ever do that to you?"

"No one cared about me. I was an orphan," I replied with a cheerless attempt at levity. "Keep going."

"If Mrs. Curtis knew, she didn't mention it. She sent me charming letters. In the summer, when they went to Cresson, she invited me to join them. My pride stopped me from revealing that I could not go where I wished. So, I sent Polly, my maid, to her aunt's in the countryside, pretended to head to Seal Harbor, and secretly went to Cresson. I did warn you this would be an unpleasant story."

I walked over and stood in front of her. All the pent-up jealousy from the past weeks had been fired by her revelations. If Sullivan had walked over the sands at that moment, I might have throttled him out of sheer hatred.

"Did you marry him?" I asked, my voice hoarse and alien to my own ears. "Just tell me that. Did you marry him?"

"No."

I exhaled deeply. "Did you care about him?"

She hesitated. "No," she eventually replied. "I didn't care for him."

I took a seat on the boat's edge and wiped my heated face. I was deeply ashamed of my behavior, yet a sense of immense relief mingled with my humiliation. If she hadn't married him and hadn't cared for him, nothing else really mattered.

"I regretted it, of course, as soon as the train left, but I had already sent a wire saying I was coming. I couldn't turn back. And once I arrived, the place was enchanting. There were no neighbors, but we fished, rode, motored, and the moonlight was like tonight."

I covered her hands, folded in her lap. "I understand," I admitted with remorse, "and people do strange things in moonlight. The moon has a hold on me tonight, Alison. If I'm acting rude, just remember that, okay?"

Her fingers remained still under mine. "So," she continued with a sigh, "I started to think that maybe I cared. Yet all the while, there was something not quite right. Every now and then, Mrs. Curtis would say or do something that jolted me, as if she momentarily dropped a mask. And there were issues with the staff, they were almost insolent. I couldn't understand. I don't recall when it finally struck me that old Baron Cavalcanti had been right about them not being my crowd. But I desperately wanted to escape, to get away."

"Obviously, they weren't your type," I exclaimed. "The man was married! That girl Jennie, a housemaid, was a spy for Mrs. Sullivan. If he had pretended to marry you, I'd have taken matters into my own hands! Not only that, but the man he killed, Harrington, was his wife's father. I'll make sure he pays for it, even if it costs me every ounce of energy and every penny I have."

I could have broken the news to her more gently, I could have softened the blow; I've never been proud of that evening on the beach. I alternated between being crude and brutish, like a hurt kid who passes on the hurt to their friend so both can cry together. And there Alison sat, pale and distant, lost for words.

"Married!" she finally whispered in a small voice. "I can't believe it's true. I... I was on my way to Baltimore to marry him myself when the train wreck happened."

"But you said you didn't care for him!" I protested, struggling to bridge the gaps in her story. And then I realized she was crying. She pulled her hand away from mine and searched for her handkerchief. Failing to find it, she accepted the one I offered her.

Slowly, from the handkerchief, she recounted a grim tale of a mountain road trip without Mrs. Curtis, of a lost path, a broken-down car, and a rainy night when she and Sullivan endlessly trudged but never made it home. She spoke of Mrs. Curtis, who suddenly became conventional and scandalized upon their return at dawn. She described her own reluctant consent to marry the scoundrel to salvage the compromising situation, and then… his sudden disappearance from the train. It was so agonizing for her, such a Heaven-sent relief for me, despite my anger towards Sullivan, that I burst into laughter. She glanced at me through her tear-dampened handkerchief.

"I know it sounds funny," she said, with a catch in her breath. "To think I nearly married a murderer… and I didn't… I'm crying out of sheer relief." Then she buried her face and cried once more.

"Please stop," I implored shakily. "I might forget I'm under a capital charge and could be arrested any moment if you keep crying like that."

Her head shot up from the handkerchief immediately. "I wanted to help," she said, "but I've only been thinking about myself! There were things I meant to tell you. If Jennie was, like you said, a spy, then I understand why she came to me just before I left. She had been packing my things, and she must have seen how distraught I was. As I was getting ready to leave, she approached me and said, 'Don't do it, Miss West, I beg you not to; you'll regret it forever.' Just then, Mrs. Curtis entered the room, and Jennie slipped away."

"That was all?"

"No. As we were passing through the station, the telegraph operator handed a message to Har—to Mr. Sullivan. He read it on the platform, and it visibly unsettled him. He pulled his sister aside, and they had an intense conversation. He looked pale, either out of fear or anger, I couldn't tell. Then, when we boarded the train, a woman dressed in black, with stunning hair, approached him on the car platform. She touched his arm and quickly pulled away. He glanced at her and then looked away, but she staggered as if he had struck her."

"Then what?" The situation was becoming clearer.

"On the train, Mrs. Curtis and I had the drawing-room. I had a dreadful night, managing only bits of sleep here and there. I dreaded to see dawn come. It was to be my wedding day. When we discovered that

Harry had vanished overnight, Mrs. Curtis was frantic. Then… I saw his cigarette case in your possession. I had given it to him. You were wearing his clothes. The murder was revealed, and you were accused! What could I do? And later, when I found him asleep in the farmhouse, I… I was overcome with panic. I locked him in and fled. I didn't understand his motive, but… he had killed a man!"

Someone was calling for Alison through a megaphone from the veranda. It sounded like Sam. "All-ee," he called. "All-ee! I'm going to have some anchovies on toast! All-ee!" Neither of us paid attention.

"I wonder," I pondered, "if you'd be willing to recount a part of that story, starting from the telegram onward, to a couple of detectives, say on Monday. If you could share that and explain how the end of your necklace ended up in the sealskin bag…"

"My necklace!" she repeated. "But it's not mine. I found it in the car."

"All-ee!" Sam's voice again. "I see you down there. I'm fixing a julep!"

Alison turned and called back through her hands. "Coming in a moment, Sam," she replied and stood up. "It must be quite late. Sam is back home. We should head inside."

"Don't," I pleaded. "Anchovies, juleps, and Sam can wait. I have so little time with you. I may be just one among many, but… you're the only girl in the world for me. You know I love you, don't you, darling?"

Sam was whistling, a maddening birdcall, repeatedly. She puckered her lips and responded in kind. It was more than I could bear.

"Sam or no Sam," I asserted resolutely, "I'm going to kiss you!"

But Sam's voice boomed through the megaphone. "Behave, you two," he shouted, "I've got the binoculars!" And so, under his watchful gaze, we strolled back to the house with a dignified attitude. My heart raced. The soft swish of her dress beside me on the grass was both agony and ecstasy. All I had to do was reach out and touch her, but I didn't dare.

Sam, armed with a megaphone and binoculars, leaned over the railing, observing us with malicious glee.

"Back already, huh?" Alison called out as we approached the steps.

"Led a club when my partner doubled no-trumps, and she fainted. Curse that heart convention!" he exclaimed with good humor. "The others haven't arrived yet."

Three hours later, I headed upstairs to sleep. I hadn't been alone with Alison since. The commotion downstairs was still going strong, and I cast a glance down into the moonlit garden. Johnson stood leaning against a tree, observing the billiard room with evident curiosity.

Chapter Twenty-Nine
IN THE DINING-ROOM

- NOTES -

CARRIAGE STEP – A carriage step is a block of stone placed near the edge of the street usually in line with the front doorway of a home. It served as a stepping stone to help passengers as they climbed in and out of carriages. Popular back in the horse and buggy days of the 19th century, carriage steps could be seen in towns and cities all over the United States. While most of carriage steps have been removed, they still exist here and there in many older towns, especially in the eastern United States.

That was Saturday night, two weeks after the accident. The preceding five days had been a whirlwind of events: the woman in the house next door, the man on the doomed train at the movie theater, dinner at the Dallases', Richey discovering Alison's involvement in the case. Then, in rapid sequence, had come our visit to the Carter place, finding the rest of the telegram, seeing Alison there, and the odd conversation with Mrs. Conway. The Cresson trip stood out in my memory for its mix of horror, humor and thrill. Then came the discovery by the police of the seal-skin bag and chain piece; Hotchkiss triumphantly presenting Stuart for Sullivan, McKnight arriving at the station with Alison, and later his confession of being out of the game.

Yet, as I reflected on the entire week and its unfolding events, everything was converging towards a decisive point. That very point was at that moment outside my window: a man sitting on a carriage step, legs stretched out, smoking a pipe. The line between the ridiculous and the tragic is very thin. I opened the window and whistled, and Johnson looked up with a grin. Without words, I offered him cigars, and he extended his hat to catch them. Eventually, I drifted to sleep in a breeze carrying the scent of salt air and fine tobacco.

My sleep was restless, my dreams featuring detectives, Hotchkiss, Alison and a short, broken chain. At dawn, a light knock woke me. It was Forbes, wearing mismatched pajamas, his grumpiness evident from having been roused from sleep. He complained about the telephone ringing for an hour, suggesting that someone else should have answered it. I left him and took the call, Richey's voice coming through, exuberant. He had found me by the simple expedient of tracing Alison, and he was jubilant.

"You need to return," he declared. "Got a train schedule handy?"

"No schedules in my pajama pocket, but stay on the line, I'll call out the window to Johnson," I quipped.

Richey's laughter echoed as I went to the window. "Train to Richmond at 6:30 AM," I announced upon my return. "What time is it now?"

"Four. Listen, Lollie. We've got him. Understand? Through the Baltimore woman. Then the other lady, the lady of the restaurant," he was clearly avoiding names, "she's playing our cards for us. No, I don't know why, don't care. Just be at the Incubator tonight, 8 PM. If you can't ditch Johnson, bring him, bless him."

To this day, I believe the Sam Forbeses haven't gotten over the surprise of my arrival, my appearance at dinner in Granger's attire and the note on my dresser the next morning, informing them that I had folded my tents like the Arabs and vanished.

By 5:30 AM, Johnson and I, he as nonchalant as ever, hit the dusty road to the station three miles away, arriving in Washington by 4 PM. The journey was uneventful; Johnson chatted about gallows improvements, regretted the loss of free passes to executions and pointed out the oddity that a man about to hang gets a hearty meal. I didn't enjoy my dinner that night.

Before reaching Washington, I cut a deal with Johnson to surrender myself at 2 PM the next day. I also sent a wire to Alison, inquiring if she'd keep her promise. The detective dropped me off at home and left. Mrs. Klopton's reception was chilly, her tone hinting at trouble.

"Now, what is it, Mrs. Klopton?" I asked, when she had informed me, in a patient and long-suffering tone, that she felt worn out and she needed a rest.

"Back when I served Mr. Justice Springer," she started sharply, mending-basket in hand, "it was an orderly house. Neighbors can confirm it. Meals were cooked and eaten, none of this 'here today, gone tomorrow' business."

"Nonsense," I rebutted. "You're just tired, Mrs. Klopton, that's all. Could you leave, now? I need to take a bath."

"That's *not* all," she asserted with dignity from the doorway. "Women coming and going, women unworthy of my shoes – I mean, who are not fit to touch my shoes – bold as brass, asking for you."

"Good Lord!" I exclaimed.

"What did you tell her… I mean them?"

"Said you were sick in a hospital, out for a year!" she declared triumphantly. "And when she suggested waiting inside, I slammed the door on her."

"When was she here?"

"Late last night. And she had a blond guy across the street. If she thinks I didn't spot him, she doesn't know me." And with that, she shut the door and left me to ponder.

At five minutes to eight, I entered the Incubator. Hotchkiss and McKnight huddled over a table, McKnight's weaponry laid out – pistols, an elephant gun, and an old cavalry saber.

"Grab a seat and help yourself to pie," he gestured towards the array of weapons. "This is for the benefit of our friend Hotchkiss here, who claims to be small and attached to life."

Hotchkiss, struggling to fit a cartridge into a revolver's barrel, straightened up and wiped his brow. "We're dealing with desperate folks," he declared with pomposity, "and we might need desperate measures."

"Hotchkiss acts like the kid whose dream was to make people tremble at the mention of his name," McKnight quipped. But beneath the banter, they were both dead serious, and after hearing their plan, so was I.

"You're compounding a felony," I objected once they laid it out. "I'm not keen on being locked up, but by Jove, to give her the stolen notes in exchange for Sullivan?"

"We don't have either of them, remember," McKnight reasoned, "and we won't unless we act. Let's go, Fido," he addressed Hotchkiss.

The plan was simple. According to Hotchkiss, Sullivan was set to rendezvous with Bronson at Mrs. Conway's apartment at 8:30 that night, with the notes. He was to be paid, and the papers destroyed. "But just before that finale," McKnight concluded, "we'll walk in, snatch the notes, apprehend Sullivan, and give the police a surprise they won't forget."

None of us had even a hint of doubt as we sped around corners in the car that night, convinced that we were on the right path, that Fate was finally favoring us. Little Hotchkiss was a bundle of nerves, alternately twitching and handling the revolver. This made me anxious, fearing they might eventually coincide. He produced and analyzed the scrap of pillowcase from the wreck, revealing the dagger with its tip wrapped in cotton batting for safekeeping. In between, he pleaded with Richey to ease off on the sharp turns.

Nevertheless, when we arrived at the building where Mrs. Conway had her apartment, our demeanor was grave and hushed. McKnight kept the engine running in case we needed a swift exit, while Hotchkiss gave a final glance to his revolver. I had no weapon; somehow, the entire scene teetered on the brink of melodrama and absurdity. In the doorway, Hotchkiss was a few steps ahead; Richey fell back to my side. He abandoned his veneer of levity, and I could see a weariness in his eyes. "Same old Sam, I guess?" he queried.

"Same, only more of him."

"I suppose Alison was here? How's she doing?" he asked offhandedly.

"She's fine. I didn't see her this morning."

Hotchkiss stood by the elevator. McKnight gripped my arm. "Listen up, buddy," he said, "I've got two arms and a revolver, and you've got one arm and a splint. If Hotchkiss is right and there's trouble, you get under a table."

"Absolutely not!" I scoffed.

Exiting the elevator on the fourth floor, we stepped into a somewhat theatrical hallway of draperies and armor. Silence enveloped us after the elevator left, and we hesitated, eyeing a few doors nearby. They were sturdy, metal-covered, and soundproof. From above came the precise sound of a player-piano, and through an open window, we could sense the thrum of the Cannonball's engine.

"So, Sherlock," McKnight quipped, "what's the next move? Ours or theirs? You led us here."

None of us had a clear plan. No sounds of conversation reached us through the heavy doors. We waited restlessly for a while, and Hotchkiss glanced at his watch. Then he held it to his ear.

"Good Lord!" he exclaimed, tilting his head, "I think it's stopped. I fear we're late."

Indeed, we *were* late. My watch and Hotchkiss' confirmed it was nine o'clock. The realization that our man might have already come and gone dampened our enthusiasm for the venture. McKnight motioned us away from the door and rang the bell, but received no response, no sound from within. He rang it twice more, the last time with urgency, to no avail. He turned to us.

"I don't like this," he admitted. "The woman is in; you heard me ask the elevator boy. I'd…"

I spotted it when he did. The door was slightly ajar, revealing a thin sliver of rose-colored light beyond. I pushed the door open slightly and listened. With both men following closely behind, I stepped into the apartment's private corridor and surveyed the area. It was a square reception hall, carpeted, with a tall mahogany hat rack and a couple of chairs. A lantern with rose-tinted glass and a desk lamp over a writing table illuminated the room, giving it a warm and inviting glow. It was empty.

We all felt uneasy. The space was filled with feminine belongings, reminding us of our vulnerability. This instinct led McKnight to suggest a split.

"We look like an invading army," he noted. "If she's alone, we'll startle her out of her wits. One of us could take a look around and…"

"Did you catch that? Didn't you hear something?"

The sound, whatever it had been, didn't repeat. Awkwardly, we stepped into the hall, all of us uneasy, and flipped a coin. The choice fell to me, which was appropriate, as the affair was primarily mine.

"Stay just inside the door," I instructed, "and if Sullivan or anyone fitting his description arrives, apprehend him immediately and ask questions later."

The apartment, except for the hallway, lay in darkness. I encountered the kitchen first, due to some peculiar modern layout, and was unexpectedly struck by a swinging door. Armed with a handful of matches, I ventured further through a butler's pantry and a refrigerator room, ending up entirely disoriented in the pitch-black darkness. Until then, it had only been an uncomfortable situation; suddenly, it turned eerie. A sustained groan echoed nearby, followed almost immediately by the crash of glass or china hitting the floor.

I struck another match, finding myself in a narrow rear hallway. The door behind me was likely the one I had entered through. Desperate to return to my starting point, I opened the door and attempted to cross the room. I thought I had kept my bearings, but I unexpectedly collided with the dining table, likely set for dinner from the ensuing cacophony. I cursed myself for getting into such a situation, and my jittery nerves for making my hand shake when I tried to strike another match. The groan had not been repeated.

Leaning against the table, I struck the match against the sole of my shoe; the flame flickered faintly before extinguishing. Then, out of nowhere, another dish crashed down from the table, splintering into a thousand pieces. The very air seemed to fracture into waves of noise. I stood still, steadying myself against the table, the dying match's end glowing red. And then, without warning, the groan resumed, and I recognized it… it was the pained cry of a distressed dog. Relief washed over me.

"Come here, buddy," I encouraged. "Come on, let's check you out."

I could hear the thump of his tail on the floor, but he remained still, whimpering. The presence of a dog is oddly comforting, and I felt for his distress. Slowly, I began to maneuver around the table toward him.

"Good boy," I said as he whimpered. "We'll find the light, it's going to be around here somewhere, and then…"

Suddenly, I tripped over something and hastily drew my foot back. "Did I step on you, buddy?" I wondered aloud, bending to pat him. I remember standing up abruptly, hearing the dog softly padding around the table toward me. I realized I had set the matches down and couldn't find them. Then, a consuming dread of the room and its contents took over me. The suffocating darkness seemed to taunt me as I desperately searched for the door I'd entered through.

I couldn't find it. My hands grazed along the unending wainscoting, tracing what seemed mile after mile of wall. The dog may have been beside me, but all I could think about was the Thing under the table. After what felt like an eternity, my trembling hand found a doorknob, and I stumbled into the reception hall. I was as nearly in a panic as any man could be.

Within moments, I had regained my composure and used the light from the hall to guide us back to the scene I had unwittingly stumbled upon.

Bronson still sat at the table, cigarette burning a hole in the cloth as he leaned on his elbows. Mrs. Conway was partly under the table, face down. The dog stood nearby, tail wagging.

McKnight silently gestured to a large copper ashtray filled with ashes and charred paper fragments. "The notes, I suppose," he commented with a tinge of regret. "He managed to get them after all, and burned them before her. She couldn't bear it. She stabbed him first, then herself."

Hotchkiss rose from his seat, removing his hat. "They're both dead," he announced solemnly, and took his notebook out of his hatband.

McKnight and I took the only course of action we could think of: we ushered Hotchkiss and the dog out of the room, then locked the door behind us.

"This is a matter for the police," McKnight asserted. "I assume you have an officer tied to you somewhere, Lawrence? You usually do."

We left Hotchkiss in charge and descended the stairs. It was McKnight who spotted Johnson leaning against a park railing across the street and waved him over. In a few succinct sentences, we relayed what we had discovered, and he grinned at me cheerfully.

"Sooner or later, in a few weeks or months, Mr. Blakeley," he said, "when you've had your fill of fooling around with the bloodstains and fingerprint expert upstairs, come to me. I've had that guy you're after under surveillance for ten days!"

Chapter Thirty
FINER DETAILS

At 1:50 PM the next day, Monday, I arrived at my office, after settling my affairs in the morning and then taking a trip to the stable. The afternoon could either make me free or a prisoner for an indefinite length of time. Despite Johnson's promise to produce Sullivan, I was more ready for the latter than the former.

Blobs was waiting for me outside, visibly excited. He simply winked, as if to say, "I'm on your side." I was too absorbed to react or respond. He followed me to the small room where we store old law books, typewriter supplies, and our coats. I was wondering if I would ever hang my coat there again, when the door closed behind me and I was left in darkness. I groped to the door irritably, and found it locked from the outside. A whisper came through the keyhole.

"Keep quiet," Blobs huskily whispered. "You're in danger. Three police officers are waiting in your office. I'm locking them in and tossing the key out the window."

"Get back here, you troublemaker!" I yelled, but he hurried away, slamming the outer office door, his usual way of announcing his presence. So, I stood in the absurd cupboard, sweating from the September heat, surrounded by the smell of old leather bindings, broken overshoes and handle less umbrellas. One minute, I seethed with anger; the next, I stifled laughter. It seemed an hour before Blobs came back, strutting with dignity, and paused by my prison door.

"That should hold them for a bit," he said, working the lock. "I've trapped them like sardines! You should have heard them!"

When he recovered from the shaking I gave him, he started to splutter. "How was I supposed to know?" he sulked. "Last time, you almost broke your neck escaping. And I don't have the old key. It's lost."

"Where's it lost?" I asked.

"Down the elevator shaft." Indignant satisfaction gleamed through his tears of humiliation.

So, while he searched for the key in the debris at the bottom of the elevator shaft, I reassured his captives, claiming the lock had jammed and they'd be free once we found the janitor with a pass-key. Stuart eventually went down and found Blobs, who had the key in his pocket, explaining to the engineer how he had tried to prevent my arrest and failed. When Stuart returned, he was almost cheerful, but Blobs didn't show up for the rest of the day.

Around the same time we found the key, Hotchkiss arrived, and we entered the room together. I shook hands with the two men. The taller one, older and stern, quickly stated his purpose.

"A warrant from Pittsburgh?" I asked, unlocking my cigar drawer.

"Yes. Allegheny County claims jurisdiction, as the exact location of the crime was in doubt," he explained as the spokesperson. The other man, shorter and plump, remained silent. "We hope you'll agree to waive extradition," he continued. "It'll save time."

"I'll come, of course," I agreed. "The sooner, the better. But give me an hour here, gentlemen. I believe we can pique your interest. Care for a cigar?"

The lean man took one, while the plump man grabbed three, putting two in his pocket.

"Any danger of the door catch going off again?" he jested, oddly cheerful given the circumstances. Hotchkiss, on the other hand, was uneasy, pacing with his hands under his coat-tails. McKnight's arrival created a diversion. He carried a long package and a corkscrew, and he shook hands with the police and effortlessly opened the bottle.

"I always need something to lift the spirits on such occasions," he remarked. "Where's the water, Blakeley? Is everyone ready?" Then he toasted the detectives in French, humorously wishing them ill. "To your eternal frustration," he said, bowing ceremoniously. "May you depart and never return! If you take Mr. Blakeley with you, I hope you choke."

The lean man nodded solemnly. "Prosit," he said, while the plump one leaned back and laughed heartily.

Hotchkiss summarized his position mentally, then set down his glass. "Gentlemen," he announced pompously, "within five minutes, the man you want will arrive, a murderer caught in a net of evidence so fine that a mosquito could not get through!"

The detectives exchanged serious glances. Had they not in their possession a sealskin bag containing a wallet and a bit of gold chain, which, by pinning the crime on me, would leave a gap large enough for Sullivan himself to slip through?

"Why not deliver your little speech before Johnson brings the other man, Lawrence?" McKnight suggested. "They won't believe you, but it might help them grasp the impending situation."

"You do realize," the lean man added gravely, "that what you say can be used against you."

"I'll take the risk," I replied impatiently.

It took a while to recount my futile trip to Pittsburgh and its aftermath. They listened attentively, without interruptions.

"Mr. Hotchkiss here," I concluded, "believes Sullivan, whom we're expecting, committed the crime. Mr. McKnight leans toward implicating Mrs. Conway, who stabbed Bronson and then herself last night. As for me, I'm open to conviction."

"That's for a jury to decide." the stout detective quipped.

And then Alison was announced. My impulse to go out and meet her was forestalled by the detectives, who rose when I did. McKnight brought her in, and I greeted her at the door.

"I've inconvenienced you," I apologized, seeing her survey the room. "I wish I hadn't…"

"It's only right that I should be here," she replied, looking up at me. "I'm afraid I'm the inadvertent cause of much of this. Mrs. Dallas will wait in the outer office."

I introduced Hotchkiss and the two detectives. They observed her with interest, likely finding her demeanor, beauty, and attire intriguing. They remained standing until she sat down.

"I've brought the necklace," she began, offering a white-wrapped box, "as you requested."

I handed it, unopened, to the detectives. "The necklace from which was broken the fragment you found in the sealskin bag," I explained. "Miss West found it on the car floor near berth lower ten."

"When did you find it?" the lean detective inquired, leaning forward.

"In the morning, shortly before the crash."

"Had you seen it before?"

"I'm not entirely sure," she answered. "I've seen one quite similar." Her tone was concerned. She looked at me for support, but I was powerless.

"Where?" The detective observed her closely. Just then, the door swung open unceremoniously, and Johnson ushered in a tall, blond man, a stranger to us all. I glanced at Alison; she was pale, yet composed and disdainful. She locked eyes with the newcomer, who, taken off guard, took a step back.

"Take a seat, Mr. Sullivan," McKnight greeted warmly. "Care for a cigar? Apologies, Alison, does the smoke bother you?"

"Not at all," she responded calmly.

Sullivan took a moment to gather himself. "No… no, thanks," he mumbled. "If you could kindly explain to me…"

"Oh, but you're here to explain to us," McKnight cheerfully interjected, pulling up a chair. "And you have a most attentive audience. These two gentlemen are Pittsburgh detectives, and we're all eager to learn the finer details of what happened on the Ontario two weeks ago, the night your father-in-law was killed. We're not biased, mind you. The Pittsburgh gentlemen are betting on Mr. Blakeley over there. Mr. Hotchkiss, the man by the radiator, is ready to bet ten to one on you. And the rest of us have our own theories."

"Gentlemen," Sullivan said slowly, "I give you my solemn word that I didn't murder Simon Harrington and I have no knowledge of who did."

"Nonsense!" Hotchkiss exclaimed, moving forward. "I can tell you…" But McKnight firmly guided him into a chair and kept him there.

"I am prepared to confess to the theft," Sullivan continued. "I took Mr. Blakeley's clothes, I admit that. If there's any way I can compensate him for the inconvenience…"

The stout detective gaped, absorbing the information. "Are you saying," he asked, "that you entered Mr. Blakeley's berth, as he claims, stole his clothes and the forged notes, and left the train before the crash?"

"Yes."

"The notes, then?"

"I handed them to Bronson yesterday. Much good they did him!" he added bitterly.

We fell into a brief silence. The two detectives were grappling with this shift in perspective. Sullivan appeared disheartened, his hands hanging loosely between his knees.

I focused on Alison; from where I stood, behind her, I could almost brush against the soft hair behind her ear.

"I have no intention of pressing any charges against you," I stated with forced politeness, although I was itching to beat him up, "if you can provide a clear account of what happened on the Ontario that night."

Sullivan lifted his weary, handsome face, surveying the room. "Haven't I seen you before?" he asked. "Weren't you an uninvited guest at the Laurels a few days – or nights – ago? Remember the incident with the cat and the rug that slipped?"

"I remember," I replied curtly.

His gaze shifted from me to Alison and quickly away. "The truth won't harm me," he said, "but it's terribly unpleasant. Alison, you're aware of all this. It's best if you leave."

His use of her name sent me into a frenzy. I stepped in front of her, looming over him. "You will not mention Miss West in this conversation," I warned, "and she will stay if she desires."

"Very well," he responded with feigned nonchalance.

Meanwhile, Hotchkiss broke free from Richey's grasp and crossed the room. "Have you ever worn glasses?" he asked eagerly.

"Never," Sullivan replied, glancing contemptuously at mine. "I'd better start by going back a bit," he continued sullenly. "You probably know I was married to Ida Harrington about five years ago. She was a good girl, and I had genuine feelings for her. However, her father opposed our marriage… He never approved of me, and he refused any kind of settlement.

"I had assumed, naturally, that there would be money, and it was a rude awakening when I realized I had miscalculated. My sister was devastated… We were broke, my sister and I."

I was watching Alison. Her hands were tightly interlocked in her lap, and she gazed out the window at the bleak rooftop below. Her lips were pressed together slightly in a subtle hint of resolve.

"Of course, you realize I'm not attempting to defend myself," the sullen voice continued. "The day came when old Harrington forced both of us out of his house at gunpoint. I threatened… I assume you're aware of that as well… I threatened to kill him.

"My sister and I faced hardships afterward. We lived on the continent for a time. I was in Monte Carlo, while she resided in Italy. She met a young woman there, the granddaughter of a steel magnate and an heiress, and she summoned me. When I reached Rome, the girl had disappeared. Last winter, I was in a tough spot. I was working as a social secretary for an Englishman, a wholesale grocer with a new title, but we had a falling out, and I returned home. I visited the Heaton boys' ranch in Wyoming, where I met Bronson. He lent me money, and since then, I've been doing his dirty work."

Sullivan rose, pacing slowly back and forth as he spoke, his gaze fixed on the faded design of the office rug. "If you wish to experience hell," he said bitterly, "put yourself at the mercy of another person. Bronson got entangled in a scheme involving John Gilmore's forged name on those notes. Somehow, he learned that a man would be bringing the papers back to Washington on the Flier. He even knew the berth number: lower ten, car seven. On the night before the crash, just as I was boarding the train, I received a telegram."

Hotchkiss stepped forward importantly. "It read something like: 'Man with papers in lower ten, car seven. Get them.'"

Sullivan regarded the little man with sulky blue eyes. "It was something like that. It was a nasty situation, worsened by the fact that Bronson didn't seem to care about the implications of a telegram that would pass through multiple hands and potentially incriminate me.

"Then, adding to my already precarious situation," Sullivan continued, "shortly after we boarded the train – I was accompanying my sister and this young lady, Miss West – a woman tapped me on the shoulder, and I turned to face… my wife!

"That stripped away my remaining courage. I confided in my sister, and you can imagine how distraught she was. We understood the implications. Ida had learned of my intentions…"

He paused and glanced uneasily at Alison.

"Go on," she said icily. "It's too late to protect me now. That should have been done when I was your guest."

"Anyway," he continued, avoiding my gaze, which likely wasn't pleasant, "Miss West was graciously considering marrying me, and…"

"You scoundrel!" I burst out, stepping past Alison's chair. "You… You despicable coward!"

One of the detectives rose and stood between us. "Mr. Blakeley, please remember that you're extracting this story from him. These details are uncomfortable but crucial. So, you were planning to marry this young lady," he turned to Sullivan, "even though you were already married?"

"It was my sister's idea, and I was in dire financial straits. If I could secretly marry a wealthy girl and go to Europe, it seemed unlikely that Ida – that is, Mrs. Sullivan – would find out.

"So it was beyond shocking to find my wife on the train, and to realize from her expression that she was aware of the situation. I still don't know how she found out, unless some of the servants... Well, that's not important now.

"It meant the whole plan had unraveled. Old Harrington had held a grudge against me for years, and there wasn't enough room on the same train for both of us. I assumed he was in the coach just behind ours."

Hotchkiss leaned forward now, his eyes narrowed, his thin lips drawn to a line. "Are you left-handed, Mr. Sullivan?" he inquired.

Sullivan paused in surprise. "No," he replied gruffly, "I can't do anything with my left hand."

Hotchkiss deflated slightly, disappointed yet attentive.

"I tore up that cursed telegram, but I was afraid to throw the scraps away. Then I looked around for berth lower ten. It was almost directly opposite – my berth was lower seven. It was, of course, exceptionally fortunate for me that the car was number seven."

"Did you inform your sister about the telegram from Bronson?" I asked.

"No, it wouldn't have helped, and she was already struggling enough without that burden," Sullivan replied.

"Your sister was killed in the wreck, I believe," the shorter detective mentioned, producing a small package from his pocket and snapping the rubber band that held it.

"Yes, she was killed," Sullivan responded somberly. "What I'm about to say can't harm her now."

He paused to push back the heavy hair falling over his forehead, then continued more coherently. "It was late, well past midnight, and we went to our berths immediately. I undressed and then lay there for an hour, pondering how to get the notes. Someone in lower nine was restless and awake, but eventually quieted down.

"The occupant of berth ten was sleeping soundly. I could hear his breathing, and it seemed like a simple matter of getting across and behind the curtains of his berth without being noticed. After that, it was mere a matter of searching for the notes surreptitiously.

"The car grew very quiet. When I was about to try for the other berth, someone brushed softly past, and I remained still. Finally, however, when things had settled down, I got up and, after glancing down the aisle, I slipped behind the curtains of lower ten. You see, Mr. Blakeley, I believed you were in lower ten, with the notes."

I nodded briefly.

"I'm not attempting to justify myself," he continued. "I was ready to steal the notes… I had no choice. But murder!"

He wiped his forehead with his handkerchief. "Well, I made my way across and behind the curtains. The man in ten didn't move. It was completely dark, and I came across a piece of chain, about the length of my finger. It was an odd thing to discover there, and it was sticky, too."

He shuddered, and I noticed Alison's hands clenching and unclenching with tension.

"All of a sudden, it struck me that the man was strangely silent, and I think I panicked. Regardless, I opened the curtains a bit to let light fall on my hands. They were red, stained with blood."

He rested one hand on the back of the chair, falling silent for a moment, as if reliving the horrifying events of that fateful night.

The stout detective had let his cigar go out, and he was drawing on it nervously. Richey had taken up a paperweight and was tossing it between his hands. When it slipped and fell to the floor, a collective shudder swept through the room.

"There was something glittering in there," Sullivan continued, "and on impulse, I picked it up. Then I let the curtains fall and stumbled back to my own berth."

"Where you wiped your hands on the bedding and stuck the dagger into the pillow," Hotchkiss added, watching his meticulously constructed framework crumble before his eyes, his expression one of chagrin.

"I suppose I did. My recollection of what happened next is rather hazy. However, when I started to regain my senses, I noticed a Russian leather wallet lying in the aisle, almost at my feet. Foolishly, I placed it in my bag, along with the bit of chain.

"I remained there, shivering, for what felt like hours. It was still eerily quiet, except for someone snoring, which felt maddening.

"The more I thought of it, the bleaker my situation appeared. The telegram was the initial strike against me, it would lead the authorities straight to me once they realized that the occupant of lower ten had been killed.

"Then I remembered the notes, so I took out the wallet and opened it."

He paused briefly, as if the recollection of the next events was almost too much to bear.

"I took out the wallet," he said simply, "and upon opening it, held it up to the light. The name 'Simon Harrington' was embossed in gold letters."

The detectives leaned forward, their focus unwavering on his face.

"Everything seemed to spin around me for a while. I sat there, nearly paralyzed, pondering what this new twist of fate meant for me.

"I knew my wife would swear that I had murdered her father; it was unlikely anyone would believe the truth.

"Do you believe me now?" He stared defiantly at us. "I am telling the absolute truth, and not a single one of you believes me!

"After a while, the occupant of berth lower nine got up and walked down the aisle, heading towards the smoking compartment. I heard his departure, and peering from my berth, I watched him disappear from view.

"It was then that I conceived the idea of swapping berths with him, donning his clothes, and escaping the train. I swear I had no intention of casting suspicion on him."

Alison's expression was scornfully skeptical, but I sensed that the man was being truthful.

"I changed the numbers of the berths, and it worked perfectly. I entered his berth, and he returned to mine. The rest was straightforward. I dressed in his clothes – luckily, they fit – and I disembarked from the train near Baltimore, shortly before the crash."

"There is another matter that requires clarification," I interjected. "Why did you attempt to call me from M——, and why did you change your mind about sending the message?"

He appeared astonished. "You knew I was in M——?" he stuttered.

"Yes, we managed to track you down. Now, about the message?"

"Well, here's how it went: I didn't know your name, Mr. Blakeley. The telegram read, 'Man with papers in lower ten, car seven.' After I thought I had successfully escaped, I began to worry about the man left in my berth. He could potentially be accused of the crime. Even though I assumed that everyone associated with the incident had perished in the crash, there was a chance you had survived. I might not have amounted to much, but I didn't want a man to suffer unjustly because I left him in my place. Furthermore, I began to have my own theory.

"As we entered the car, a tall, dark-haired woman passed us, holding a glass of water. I had a vague recollection of her; she bore a striking resemblance to Blanche Conway.

"If she also believed that the man with the notes was in lower ten, it would explain a lot, including that fragment of a necklace. Blanche Conway was a woman capable of anything."

"Then, why did you cancel the message?" I inquired with curiosity.

"After I reached the Carter house and got into bed – I had sprained my ankle jumping off the train – I rummaged through the alligator bag I took from lower nine. Upon finding your name, I sent the initial message. Shortly afterward, I stumbled upon the notes. It seemed too good to be true, and I was consumed with fear that the message had already been dispatched.

"Initially, my intention was to deliver the notes to Bronson. Yet, I began to understand the significance of possessing those notes. They represented power over Bronson, money, influence… everything. I needed something, some sort of leverage. That man was a devil."

"Well, then, I suppose he's right at home now." McKnight interjected, prompting us to break into laughter and alleviate some of the tension.

Alison shielded her eyes, seemingly trying to block out the sight of the man she had nearly married, while I discreetly touched one of the soft curls nestled at the nape of her neck.

"When I regained my ability to walk," the sullen voice continued, "I immediately made my way to Washington. I attempted to sell the notes to Bronson, but he was almost at the end of his rope. Even my threat to return the notes to you, Mr. Blakeley, failed to sway him to meet my demands. He didn't have the money."

McKnight wore a triumphant expression. "I believe my theory is making sense now, gentlemen," he declared. "Mrs. Conway sought the notes to force a legal marriage, I presume?"

"Yes."

The detective with the small package carefully rolled off the rubber band and unwrapped it. He took out, first, the Russia leather wallet. "Mr. Blakeley, we discovered these items in the bag Mr. Sullivan alleges he left with you. Mr. Sullivan, is this the wallet you found on the car's floor?"

Sullivan opened the wallet and, upon seeing the name engraved inside, "Simon Harrington," he nodded in affirmation.

"And this," the detective continued, "is the piece of gold chain?"

"It appears to be," Sullivan responded, recoiling at the sight of the blood-stained end.

"This, I believe, is the dagger." the detective said, and he held it up. Alison let out a soft cry of astonishment and dismay. Sullivan's complexion turned pallid, and he sank weakly onto the nearest chair.

The detective observed him keenly before shifting his gaze to Alison's visibly agitated expression. "Young lady," he addressed her kindly, "have you seen this dagger before?"

"Oh, please don't make me say it!" she exclaimed breathlessly, her eyes fixed on Sullivan. "It's… It's too horrifying!"

"It will come out eventually," I advised, leaning in closer to her. "You might as well tell him now."

"Ask him," she replied, nodding in Sullivan's direction. The detective carefully unwrapped the small box that Alison had brought, revealing the trampled necklace and broken chain. With somewhat clumsy movements, he spread it out on the table and matched the fragment of chain to its rightful place. There was no doubt that they belonged together.

"Where did you find that chain?" Sullivan asked hoarsely, for the first time directing his gaze towards Alison.

"On the floor, near the berth of the murdered man."

"Now, Mr. Sullivan," the detective said politely, "in light of these two pieces of evidence, I believe you are capable of disclosing the identity of Simon Harrington's actual murderer."

Sullivan's eyes returned to the dagger, a slender piece of steel with a Florentine handle. He then picked up the locket and discreetly pressed a concealed mechanism beneath one of the cameos. Inside, meticulously engraved, were a name and a date.

"Gentlemen," he spoke, his face ashen, "there is no point in my attempting to deny it any longer. The dagger and necklace belonged to my sister, Alice Curtis!"

Chapter Thirty-One

AND ONLY ONE ARM

Hotchkiss broke the tension first. "Mr. Sullivan," he suddenly asked, "was your sister left-handed?"

"Yes."

Hotchkiss closed his notebook and looked around triumphantly. We all exchanged relieved smiles. After all, Mrs. Curtis was deceased, offering the most positive resolution to the unfortunate affair. McKnight brought Sullivan some whisky, and he partly regained his composure.

"I discovered from news articles that my wife was in a Baltimore hospital. I visited her yesterday, hoping her support would keep me on track. With her father and my sister both gone, we might finally find happiness together.

"Now I understand what puzzled me then. My sister entered the next car and attempted to persuade my wife not to meddle. But Ida – Mrs. Sullivan – remained steadfast, asserting her father possessed papers, certificates and the like, that could annul the marriage immediately.

"She also disclosed her father's presence in our car, hinting at trouble the next morning. It's likely my sister's attempt to secure the papers roused him, leading to the unfortunate outcome."

It was finally over. Barring a few formalities, my freedom was restored. Alison quietly prepared to depart. The men made way for her except for Sullivan, who remained hunched over in his chair, his face buried in his hands. Hotchkiss, who had been tapping his pencil on the desk, abruptly raised his gaze and pointed the pencil at me.

"If this is all true, and I believe it is… Then who was in the house next door, Blakeley, the night you and Mr. Johnson searched it? You recall mentioning a woman's hand at the trap door…"

I quickly glanced at Johnson, whose expression remained impassive. With his hand on the doorknob, he opened the door before responding. "Mrs. Conway had numerous scratches on her right hand," he said, addressing the room. "Her wrist was bandaged and badly bruised." He went out then, giving me a parting look half-amused and half-contemptuous.

McKnight escorted Alison and Mrs. Dallas to their carriage, and came back. The office gathering dispersed. Sullivan, appearing weary and aged, stood by the window, looking at the broken necklace in his hand. Upon noticing my gaze, he placed it on the desk and picked up his hat.

"If I can't do anything more…" he hesitated.

"I think you've done enough," I replied grimly, and he left.

I think Richey and Hotchkiss took me out somewhere to dinner, and later, perhaps out of concern for my loneliness, they sent for Johnson. I vaguely remember a lively debate in which Hotchkiss told the detective that he was good at handling certain cases but lacked insight. Richey and I were mostly silent, my thoughts skipping ahead to the evening's anticipated moment when I would see Alison again.

I dressed hastily, focusing intently on my tie, much to the despair of Mrs. Klopton. "Until your arm heals, it might be better to get the kind that hooks on," she protested, nearly in tears. "I'm sure they look very nice, Mr. Lawrence. My late husband always…"

"That's a lover's knot you've tied," I snapped, hastily undoing the bow she had painstakingly created. I then looked out the window for Johnson, only to remember that he was no longer part of my view. I ended up driving frantically to the club, where I asked George to assist me.

I was late, of course. The drawing-room and library at the Dallas house were empty. The sound of billiard balls echoed from somewhere, and I went in the opposite direction. Eventually, I found Alison on the balcony, seated much like she had been on the beach that night, with her chin in her hands, gazing blankly at the trees and lights in the square beyond. She was softly whistling a tender tune, but not a sad one this time. As I stood next to her, gazing down, all the myriad words I had waited to say deserted me, leaving me speechless. Moonlight cast fleeting glimmers on her hair, her eyes, her dress.

"Don't do that," I said unsteadily. "You… You know what I want to do when you whistle!"

She looked up at me, and she continued to whistle. Softly, a bit tremulously. Instantly, I forgot the street, the potential onlookers, the voices inside the house.

"The world only holds you for me," I said reverently. "It's our world, darling. I love you."

And I kissed her.

A boy was whistling on the pavement below. Reluctantly, I released her and settled back where I could see her. "I haven't gone about this the way I intended," I admitted. "In books, everything gets sorted out, and then they kiss the lady."

"Sorted out?" she questioned.

"Oh, about getting married and such," I explained casually. "We could go to Bermuda, or Jamaica… perhaps in December."

She withdrew her hand and confronted me directly.

"I believe you are afraid!" she accused. "I won't marry you unless you propose properly. It's a tradition, a woman's right, something to cherish."

"Alright," I conceded with a dramatic sigh. "If you promise not to think I'm a fool, I'll do it, even on one knee."

I had to walk past her to close the door behind us. As I kissed her again, she protested that we weren't truly engaged yet.

Turning to face her, I said triumphantly, "It's quite a predicament, loving you as much as I do, and having only one arm!" Then I shut the door.

From across the street, a sharp crescendo whistle pierced the air, and a vaguely recognizable figure detached itself from the park railing.

"Hey," he called out in a raspy whisper, "should I drop the key down the elevator shaft?"

The End

www.ingramcontent.com/pod-product-compliance
Lightning Source LLC
Chambersburg PA
CBHW031751200726
48289CB00013B/784